I0744760

THE RAVENS & THE MYSTERIOUS TOWN

(THE FALLING, #2)

JESSICA SORENSEN

The Ravens & the Mysterious Town
Jessica Sorensen
All rights reserved.
Copyright © 2019 by Jessica Sorensen
This is a work of fiction. Any resemblance of characters to actual persons, living or dead, is purely coincidental. The author holds exclusive rights to this work. Unauthorized duplication is prohibited. No part of this book can be reproduced in any form or by electronic or mechanical means including information storage and retrieval systems, without the permission in writing from the author. The only exception is by a reviewer who may quote short excerpts in a review.
Any trademarks, service marks, product names or names featured are assumed to be the property of their respective owners, and are used only for reference. There is no implied endorsement if we use one of these terms.

ISBN: 9781939045362

For information: jessicasorensen.com
Cover Design by MaeIDesign

 Created with Vellum

1

RAVEN

"You got that right swing down, right?" my dad asks as we cruise down the road in his old Camaro, music blasting from his iPod shuffle, his "old man music," as my mom calls it, playing from some speakers sitting on the back seat.

He's been working on fixing the car up but hasn't gotten very far yet. The leather seats are torn, the outside is primed but not painted, and the stereo is missing.

The windows are down, letting the warm summer breeze gust into the cab, blowing strands of my hair into my face as I nod and raise a fist in front of me. "Like this?" I swing against the air, hoping I've got the right form.

My dad smiles as he lifts his hand for a high-five, and I smile proudly as I tap my palm against his.

"That's the perfect form." He removes his cigarette from between his lips then ashes it out the window. "Keep it up and you might just end up becoming a fighter when you grow up."

"Like Momma?" I ask, crossing my fingers he'll say yes.

My momma is the coolest person I know. She's so tough. A lot of people think she's my sister, but my momma tells me that they only think that because she had me when she was young. I'm not even sure why anyone thinks she's related to me at all. She has blonde hair, where I have black; our eyes are different colors; and unlike hers, my cheeks are covered in freckles. I don't like my freckles that much. A lot of kids tease me about them. They say I look like I have dirt on my face.

"Yep, just like your momma." Dad puts his cigarette out in the ashtray then looks in the rearview mirror, messing with his scraggly brown hair.

My dad doesn't like to dress up. He wears a lot of old T-shirts and jeans. But today, he put on nice pants and a button-down shirt. He also made me wear a dress, which yuck, I hate dresses. The one I'm wearing right now is black. I'm glad for that because I hate bright colors, like pink, even more than I hate dresses. But I still don't get why he made me wear a dress or why my mom braided my *hair. They usually let me do whatever I want. Today, though, they were all about me being on my best behavior while we go to wherever the heck we're going. My dad has also checked to make sure I remember how to swing a punch, like, a ton of times.*

I don't know why he's asking this so much. I'm the only seven-year-old I know who knows how to throw a wicked right hook. I even got suspended from school once for hitting another kid. He deserved it for pantsing me. My parents thought so, too, and argued with the principal about it, which is why I no longer go to that school. Well, that and we moved recently.

The move had to do with me getting into the fight. At least, that's what I think I heard my parents whispering about late one night when they thought I was asleep. They were worried about me getting in too much trouble and drawing too much attention.

"All right, here we go," my dad mumbles as he pulls up to a set of tall gates.

We've been driving for what feels like hours and, until this gate, I haven't seen anything other than fields, trees, and old gas stations.

"Where are we?" I ask, kneeling up in the seat to try to see over the gates, but there are too many trees in my way.

Dad pushes the shifter into park and stares at the gates

with a frown on his face. He's not usually the kind of guy who frowns a lot, so it's weird to see one on his face.

"Dad?" I say when he doesn't seem like he's going to answer me. "What is this place?"

He glances at me. "This, Ravenlee, is a stipulation."

"Am I in trouble?" I ask, glancing at the gate again. He only calls me Ravenlee when he's mad at me or stressed out.

He shakes his head. "No, you're not in trouble. If anything, I am."

"Why?"

He shrugs. "I don't know ... It's ..." He offers me a smile. "You don't need to worry about it. This is grown up stuff. All you need to worry about today is making sure that, if anything bad happens, you swing your fist like your life depends on it, got it?"

I nod, wanting to make him proud of me. "Got it."

He starts to smile, but it fades when the gates start to open.

Sighing, he drives forward through the entrance and turns onto a paved driveway that leads to the biggest house I've ever seen.

"Whoa, who lives here?" I ask with my nose pressed against the window.

The house is so huge that it has three floors.

"A business acquaintance," my dad replies as he pulls up to the front doors.

Two guys are standing on the front porch, and just behind them is a kid around my age with dark brown hair. Even with how far away he is, I can tell he looks sad.

I turn to my dad. "Is that boy your business acquaintance?"

Shaking his head, he puts the shifter into park, turns off the engine, and then hesitantly reaches for the door. "No."

He's being really weird. It makes me worry, even though he said I don't need to. I want to ask him questions, but he opens the door and climbs out.

I'm not sure if I'm supposed to follow him or if I should stay in the car.

"Come on, Ravenlee," he says then closes the door.

He called me Ravenlee again.

Something's wrong.

But I get out anyway, trusting my dad, and hurry around to the front of the car where he's waiting for me. He takes my hand when I reach him then pulls me with him as he starts up the pathway toward the guys.

"You made it," the taller one says to my dad. Then his gaze flits to me. "And you brought her."

My dad's hold on my hand tightens. "I didn't really have a choice, did I?"

The man stares at me for a beat with eyes a strange color of grey, like storm clouds, then he looks at my dad. "No, you didn't." Again, the man with stormy eyes glances at me.

He's starting to make me feel really squirmy, so I look at the boy instead. He has a scar on his jaw. I wonder where he got it from.

He looks even sadder up close, so I smile at him. But all he does is stare at me like I'm a weirdo, which I guess I sort of am. Then his confusion shifts to worry as the man with stormy grey eyes looks at him.

"Kid, go inside and get the others," he tells him.

The kid nods then looks at me for a fleeting moment before hurrying inside the house.

The man looks back at my dad and opens his mouth to say something when lightning snaps across the sky and thunder immediately follows, so I miss what he says.

As the land shadows over with clouds and the wind picks up, the memory swirls away with it—

My eyelids pop open as I suck in a sharp breath. My skin is damp with sweat, my hair feels gross again, and the wound on my side throbs as I stare up at my bedroom ceiling.

That dream I just had ... or memory ... whatever it was ... that kid in it ... was that *Zay?* Hunter told me that Zay's dad calls him Kid, and Zay has a scar on his jawline, just like the kid did. But, why would I suddenly remember that I met Zay a long time ago?

Maybe it was just a dream. I've had vivid dreams before. But I've also forgotten memories before.

"No, it has to be a dream," I mutter to myself. There's no way I met Zay once and somehow forgot about it.

Doubt weighs on my mind, though.

Since it's still too early to get up, I close my eyes and shut my mind off, trying desperately to fall back asleep so I don't feel the pain in my side.

Last night, I took a shower to try to scrub the wound clean ... and wash the river scent out of my hair. Then I put some peroxide on the wound my uncle had given me so it wouldn't get infected before I closed my eyes, but I didn't go downstairs to pop some painkillers, not wanting to cross paths with anyone. I'm not sure if my aunt knows what my uncle did to me—if she's aware of any of the stuff he's done to me—but my bet is she does. It makes me hate her. It makes me hate my uncle.

I have a lot of hate in me right now. In fact, it burns almost as badly as the cut on my side.

Disappointment.

I roll over, trying to move away from the pain of that word, and focus again on sleeping ...

I'm in a large room with a massive, domed ceiling and a huge light decorated with crystals hanging from it. I feel in awe as I take everything in: the paintings on the walls, the fireplace, the way the air smells like cinnamon.

"This place is so big," I tell my dad as I turn in a circle, taking everything in.

He nods, seemingly distracted as he glances at his phone. "Yeah, I know it is, Ravenlee."

He's called me Ravenlee three times since we arrived at this strange house in the middle of nowhere and hasn't given me an explanation as to why we're here. The large guys who greeted us at the entryway led us into this room before wandering off after telling us not to go anywhere.

I haven't seen the scarred boy that one of the men called "Kid" since he wandered into the house. Honestly, I haven't seen anyone besides my dad since the men left us here. I haven't heard anything either.

This place is spookily quiet.

I chew on my thumbnail. "How long do we have to stay here?"

"I'm not sure." His frown deepens as he reads something on the screen, worry written all over his face.

"Daddy?" I ask, starting to get really worried. "What's wrong?"

He glances up at me, his face really pale. "Ravenlee, I'm so sorry that this ..." He trails off as a tall man with dark hair enters the room. Then he swallows hard.

Something's very wrong.

"I'm glad to see you made it," the man says to my dad then glances at me in a way that makes my skin crawl.

"Did I really have a choice?" Dad mutters in an annoyed tone.

"No, but some men in your position might do something stupid, like try to run," the man replies. "Glad to see you aren't one of those men. I didn't particularly feel like chasing anyone down today." He glances at me again with a curious look on his face.

Wanting him to stop looking at me, I inch behind my dad.

A trace of a smile touches the man's lips, as if my move amuses him. "She's afraid of me," he muses. "Smart girl."

As a cold chill rolls through my body, I grab my dad's hand. "Daddy?" I whisper. "Why does he want me to be afraid of him?"

He grips my hand tightly in a reassuring squeeze. "Don't worry about it." He sounds the complete opposite of his words.

The air grows quiet as the man sinks into silence, staring at me like I'm a complex puzzle he desperately wants to solve.

"We should get this done," he finally says, looking at my dad. "Leave the girl here and come join me in my office for a drink. I'll have Kid brought in."

I have no idea what's going on, but I grasp my dad's hand desperately. "Don't leave me," I beg.

He glances down at me with remorse in his eyes. "I'm sorry, Ravenlee." Then he pries my hand out of his. "Stay here," he orders in a cold tone I've never heard him use before.

Tears burn my eyes as he starts to walk away.

When he notices I'm about to cry, he sighs, walks back to me, and crouches down so his gaze is level with mine. "Suck it up, Ravenlee," he says in a quiet but firm tone. "Crying makes us weak. Do you want to be weak, or do you want to be strong like your mom and me?"

I shake my head and sniffle, trying to suck back the tears. "Strong."

He offers me a small but sad smile. "Good girl." Then he stands up and walks away without a glance back.

I watch him leave with my fingers curled into fists and my stomach winding into knots, but my eyes are dry.

Once the man and my dad leave the room, I move to sit down on the sofa, not sure what I'm supposed to do. But before I can sit completely down, the door is opened and a woman with long, red hair walks in. She's wearing a black dress, a lot of sparkly jewelry, and her hair is done up like she's going someplace fancy. She's also not alone.

The sad boy with the scar trails in behind her, the boy

everyone keeps referring to as Kid. He looks even sadder than before, which doesn't even seem possible.

As the woman with the red hair walks toward me, she assesses me with a curious look on her face, like I'm some weird creature she's never seen before.

"So, you're the little girl everyone's been fussing over?" She stops in front of me and tilts her head. "Honestly, I don't see what the big deal is. You don't even look like her. Makes me wonder if you're really hers or if he was just bullshitting everyone. He does have a reputation for being a liar."

"So do you, Diane," the boy says with a shake of his head.

Her lips twitch in annoyance. "You little shit ..." She trails off, putting on a sugary sweet smile. "You know what? Say whatever you want about me. At least I'm not a monster."

The kid smashes his lips together, his gaze shifting to me, and I swear I see remorse in his eyes.

"What's going on?" I speak. "Who are you guys? And where's my dad?"

The woman's attention returns to me, the smile still on her face. "What's going on is that you're about to pay your whore of a mother's debt."

Anger burns under my skin as I curl my hand into a fist. "Don't call my mother that!"

The woman smirks at the sight of my balled-up fist. "Are you seriously thinking about hitting me? You're just a kid—"

I step forward and punch her in the stomach.

She grunts, her face contorting in pain. "You little brat," she seethes then starts to storm toward me.

"Diane," Kid calls out. "If you touch her, the bosses are gonna be pissed off."

She slams to a halt, breathing furiously as she glares at me then at Kid. "Fuck off," she spats but doesn't move toward me again.

Bosses? What does that mean?

I'm about to ask when the woman suddenly relaxes, the tension leaving her body.

"You know what? I don't need to listen to this shit. I was told to bring you here and nothing more." She turns, her heels clicking against the marble floor as she starts to leave. "You know what to do," she says as she passes Kid, and he visibly tenses.

Smirking, she strolls out of the room and shuts the door behind her.

Silence stretches between us as Kid just stands there with his hands balled into fists and his gaze fastened on the floor.

Finally, I can't take the silence anymore. "Your name's Kid, right?" I ask.

Shaking his head, he looks up at me. "No."

"Oh." I'm so confused. "But everyone keeps calling you that?"

"I know," he says flatly.

"Why do they call you that if it's not your name?"

He shrugs, not saying a word, just staring at me.

The silence is making me uncomfortable, so I try to think of something to say to him.

"Well, my name's Ravenlee," I tell him. "But almost everyone calls me Raven."

He studies me for a moment. "I have a pet raven."

"Really?" I ask, stepping toward him. "How the heck did you get one of those for a pet?"

He lifts a shoulder. "I caught it."

"That's really cool. Is it here? Maybe you can show it to me."

He shakes his head. "It's at my house."

"This isn't your house?" I ask, and he shakes his head. "Whose is it?"

He frowns. "The boss's."

"Who the heck is that?"

He seems to grow nervous, scratching the back of his neck. "No one you want to know."

"Oh." I pause. "Do you know why I'm here?"

He swallows hard, not answering me. It grows quiet again, and that sad look returns to his face.

Honestly, the only time he didn't look sad was when he was talking about his pet raven.

"Um ... What's your raven's name?" I ask, hoping he'll relax again and maybe tell me why the heck I'm at this house.

He lifts a shoulder. "I haven't named it."

"Well, you should," I say. "Every pet needs a name."

"Giving names to things make us weak," he mutters automatically.

"No way," I disagree, stepping toward him. "Naming things is really fun, especially pets, because you can name them just about anything. Like this one time I named this stray cat Cat. Although, he wasn't really my pet. He just wandered into my backyard sometimes."

"You named a cat Cat?" he questions.

I shrug, smiling a bit. "I thought it was funny."

"And you like to be funny?" He seems confused by this.

I shrug again. "I like to be a lot of things, but yeah, I like being funny sometimes ... Why do you seem so confused about that?"

He lifts a shoulder, staring at me like he's completely mystified. "It's just that you ... I don't know ... You seem ... happy?"

"And that's confusing?"

He shrugs again.

The boy really likes to shrug.

"Well, I am happy sometimes," I inform him. "Just like I'm sad sometimes. And angry. And scared. That's totally normal."

A crinkle forms between his brows. "Not in my world." Then he sighs loudly. "Look, I can't name my raven anything or else my dad will get mad at me."

"Really?" I ask, and he nods. "Your dad's really strict then."

"Yeah, he is," he agrees in a hollow tone.

I get the feeling his dad is a really mean guy. No wonder he looks so sad all the time.

I find myself wanting to make him happy, like I am sometimes.

An idea comes to me then. A pretty awesome one, too.

"Well, maybe you can give it a name without him knowing," I suggest. "Like how I named my cat Cat."

He gives me a funny look. "You think I should name my raven Raven?" he questions. "Like, after you?"

I give an innocent shrug, pretending like that just occurred to me. "Well, you really don't have to name it after me. It could just be a weird coincidence that we have the same name."

He sinks into silence again, giving me a suspicious look. But then the look fades. "I'll think about it."

I nod, smiling to myself. For a crazy second, he looks as

if he's smiling, too. But the look swiftly erases and fills with panic as an intercom inside the room clicks on.

"Kid, stop fucking around and do what you're supposed to," a male's voice floats from the speaker.

Kid swallows hard. "I'm sorry," he whispers then steps toward me.

My heart rate quickens, and I'm not sure why. Then he touches my arm and I hear the flapping of wings—

I gasp, my eyelids popping open.

"Holy shit," I breathe out as I sit up in bed, my scars and fresh wounds throbbing as the images of the dream linger in my mind like a bad hangover.

My stomach churns just trying to think about it, so I get up and run to the bathroom to vomit. But my stomach is empty, so I spend the next few minutes dry heaving. Then I sink down onto the floor, my skin damp with sweat, my body and soul hurting for reasons my mind won't allow me to comprehend.

What was that dream? Who is this Kid I keep dreaming of? I'm not sure, but I'm having a really hard time convincing myself that it was just a dream.

With him having that scar ... and the nickname Kid ... and a pet raven ... could my forgotten memories be resurfacing?

But that leaves me with a ton of questions. Like, why am I suddenly remembering Zay? And, does he remember me? If he does, why didn't he say anything? And what the hell happened in that room that had—and still has—me feeling like I'm going to throw up?

I press the heel of my hand to my forehead. "What the fuck happened to me?" I whisper, trying to dig out the full memory from my mind. But, just like when I killed my parents, it's like a door slams shut and locks, refusing to let me in.

Refusing to let me see the truth.

A truth that I have a feeling is horrifying.

I LIE IN BED FOR QUITE A WHILE, JUST STARING UP AT the ceiling and thinking. I have no plans of moving anytime soon until I hear the strangest noise coming from outside. It almost sounds like a fire is crackling.

Confused, I get up, tiptoe over to the window, and peer outside, surprised to find that, yep, the noise is indeed exactly what I thought it was.

A fire is crackling in the middle of the field beside my house. A man stands beside it. A man who looks an awful lot like my uncle. And what's even more creepy is I can make out a few silhouettes of some people standing behind him and the shadows of birds circle his head.

What the actual fuck?

I watch from the window as he throws something into the flames then steps back. The silhouettes move, too, walking into the darkness until I can no longer see them. Soon after, the birds fly away.

Seriously, what the actual fuck?

And what in the hell is my uncle burning in the middle of the night? Whatever it is, it can't be good. Why else would anyone burn something in the middle of the night?

My best bet is that it might be some incriminating evidence against him; proof that he's been stealing drugs from raids. I'm not sure, though.

I stand by the window for a bit, watching as he remains in front of the flames. Eventually, he puts the fire out by shoveling dirt onto it. Then he starts back toward the house.

I hunker down to avoid being seen. Then, when I hear the front door creak open, I crawl back toward my bed and climb in. And it's a good thing I do, too.

Moments later, my bedroom door is opened.

I keep my eyes shut, but I can sense someone looking at me. It has to be my uncle, but what the hell is he doing?

My side aches as worry creeps through me. What if he's contemplating cutting me again?

Eventually, though, he leaves my room.

I let out a shaky breath.

And they say I'm the weirdo. I'm not the one creeping around at night, burning things in the yard in the middle of the night with an audience, and peeping in on people.

But what the hell was he burning? And who were those people watching him? I really wish I knew. The only answer probably lies in the ashes now, resting in the dirt.

2

HUNTER

I woke up this morning with a major headache, and the strangest feeling I dreamt about something important last night. I can't remember what, though. And when I woke up, I had the strangest feeling that someone was watching me from the shadows of my room, but when I got up and checked, no one was around.

That's not too weird for me. I haven't been able to remember my dreams for years now, and I often wake up with a paranoid feeling that I'm not alone. I told a therapist about it once, and he tried to come up with a reason why. He never did give me a diagnosis, and I stopped going to him after only a few sessions, after he tried to convince me that I used sex and drugs as a coping mechanism for the bad shit that has happened to me. I mean, he was totally right, but he also tried to convince me that I needed to stop doing drugs and having sex, something I never plan on doing. Doing so means facing the fuckedupness that is my past, and again, I can't do that.

In fact, I have a routine to make sure that that never happens. I get up in the morning and cut a few lines. Then I suck them up and let them numb that fuckedupness right out of me. It's only a temporary solution, though, which is why, at the end of the day, I'll hook up with someone. Only then will I feel in control over my life again. Only then will I feel free of my past. Only then will I feel free of everyone. Everyone who ruined me.

By the time I leave my bedroom, I'm feeling pretty damn good as I head toward the workout room where I can hear someone beating the hell out of a punching bag. My bet is it's Zay.

"What the hell's your deal this morning?" I ask as I enter the room, watching as he beats the shit out of the punching bag. "You look stressed as fuck. And you never look stressed when you're hitting things." My lips quirk as I sit down on a stool and cross my arms. "It's why everyone thinks you're a psychopath."

"That's because I am." He takes a swing at the bag again. Then he tears off his gloves off and grabs a bottle of water from the mini-fridge.

I grin musingly. "Aren't we all psychopaths?"

"Yeah, we are," he agrees, taking long gulp of water.

I lean forward and rest my arms on my knees. "But, for reals, why're you so worked up this morning? Is it because of that thing you agreed to do to Raven last night?" Again, as I utter the words aloud, I feel the briefest flicker of guilt.

He shakes his head. "No."

I eye him over, knowing he's lying by how tense he is. "Since when do we lie to each other, man?"

"I'm not lying." He puts the cap back on the water bottle then heads out of the room.

I can tell something is really bothering him and I need to get to the bottom of it before he does something bad.

"Zay," I call out. "Whatever it is, man, you need to tell me. I don't want to pull a Jax and remind you of the rules, but I'm not gonna just let you silently stress out about shit either... We both know what happens when you refuse to deal with shit—you fucking explode and either you or someone else ends up getting hurt." I give a pressing glance at the bag on the floor and then at his arms, where I know he probably has cut marks on his flesh. "And considering the fact that you're wearing a long-sleeved shirt right now and moving really stiffly, I'm gonna guess that you've already taken it out on yourself a little bit."

He grits his teeth. "Yeah, so what if I did? I don't feed me any bullshit about the rules. We both know you don't give a shit about them. Not really, anyway."

I smile, but it's totally fake. "Funny, but I'm pretty sure I said something similar to you last night when Jax set the rules about our Raven."

"You need to stop calling her ours," he tells me with annoyance.

I smirk. "Not gonna happen." No, I like the sound of it way too much. Although, a small part of me wants to call her mine, but the feeling is so damn weird since I've never been the possessive type. "Now tell me what's wrong."

Zay shakes his head, looking beyond annoyed. "Look, there's nothing really bothering me. I just ... I don't know ... I feel like I know Raven from somewhere, but I have no fucking idea why."

"Really?" I frown.

Holy effing shit.

"Why don't you look that surprised?" he asks me suspiciously.

I shake my head. "Because ... I swear it feels like I know her, too."

Suddenly, those little white lines purring inside me start to silence and worry pricks its way to the surface.

"How could we possibly both feel like we know her?" I lean back and rake my fingers through my hair, tension working its way through my body.

Fuck, I really wish I'd done a few more lines.

Maybe I will before we leave ...

"I have no idea." He cracks his knuckles and bounces his leg up and down, revealing his anxiety.

I eye him over, wondering if he's keeping something from me. "You have no memories of her at all?"

He shakes his head, his gaze dissecting me as carefully as mine is him. "But my mind's shit when it comes to memories. Yours, however ..." He cocks a brow at me.

"I just have a feeling ..." I trail off. "Or, well, there is one thing."

When I give a short pause, he grows impatient. "Just spit it out, brother," he snaps, scratching his forehead.

"I'm not sure what it means," I start. "Or if it means anything. But, when Raven was standing on the bridge, surrounded by snow, looking so fucking gorgeous, I swear ... well, I swear I've seen that exact moment before. It wasn't like I was remembering an old memory. It was almost like a photograph inside my head." When he gives me a confused look, I shrug. "I know it sounds weird. That's why I was so hesitant to tell you."

Zay restlessly taps his foot against the mats covering the floor. "You think we know her somehow?"

I shake my head. "Doubtful. I mean, how could we know her yet neither of us can actually remember anything about her? More than likely, she probably just looks like someone we know." But I feel like I'm lying when I say the words aloud.

Zay massages his knuckles, staring off into space for a moment. "She has a really unique look about her, though. I mean, that hair and those eyes ... the violet tints in both ... that's kinda rare."

I've spent a lot of time photographing people to know he's right. In fact, the first time I ever laid eyes on Raven, I wanted to photograph her. And not just because she's gorgeous, but because she has such a unique look about her. And those haunted eyes of hers ... Fuck, they'd make for an amazing, emotional photo.

One of these days, I'm going to talk her into letting me photograph her.

I shake my head. Shit, I'm already getting obsessed. I can't let Jax know, or he's going to set more rules.

"What do you think we should do?" Zay asks, yanking me from my thoughts.

I shrug. "I'm not sure if we should do anything yet. Not unless one of us actually remembers why the hell she looks familiar."

Zay's brows knit. "You think we should tell Jax?"

"Tell me what?" Jax appears in the doorway. As always, his expression is neutral.

He's a scary motherfucker. At least to people outside our group. Zay and I, though, know how to handle him.

We also know that, despite the fact that he comes off as a psychopath most of the time, there's more to Jax. Don't get me wrong; he's a crazy bastard. He tries really hard to be that way, though. Deep down, I know he feels things. He just buries them with alcohol, like I bury my past with drugs and sex, just like Zay buries his rage and loss of control issues with fighting and cutting.

Yeah, we're a really messed-up circle, The Raven Three. And I have a feeling we're about to become even more messed up when we officially become The Raven Four, because I don't believe for a second that someone like Raven, who's beautiful and wild but just as crazy and unstable as the rest of us, is somehow going to balance out all of our issues and make us a stable group. Besides, in our own way, we have stability. It just lies in drugs, alcohol, fighting, pain, and sex.

"It's nothing really," I tell Jax with a shrug. "Zay and I were just talking about how there's a familiarity to our Raven, but neither of us can actually remember meeting her, so it's probably nothing."

He puts his thinking face on, which honestly isn't that much different than all his other expressions. I just know him well enough that I can see the difference.

He remains silent for a second before straightening from the doorway and entering the room. "We'll look into it more." He stops in the middle of the room. "Right now, we need to focus on getting her into our circle so we can find out what she's hiding in there." He briefly hesitates, which is weird for him. "I also think it might be a good idea to have her move in with us."

Zay gapes at him. "You want her to move in with us? Are you fucking crazy?"

"You know I am," Jax replies. "And while I'm not thrilled about the idea of having some crazy, broken girl living with us, I think it's the best way to learn more about her. And not just for our bosses, but because we need her help with something."

"With what?" Zay and I ask at the same time, both of us looking totally confused. Then again, we never get help from anyone but each other, so this is really strange.

He wavers for a second. "With getting dirt on Porter Aversonly."

Porter Aversonly is a nephew of one of our bosses' rivals. He's also in the same grade as us. The bosses gave us an order about a month ago to make friends with him so we can find out more about what the Aversonlys have been up to, since they've been really quiet over the last handful of months. And a mafia family being quiet is never a good thing.

The problem is Porter is an asshole and making friends with him is complicated since rival families don't really associate with each other. Still, we've been trying.

It's why I joined the basketball team—because Porter is on it and we thought maybe I could try to make friends with him that way. I hate playing, although I'm good at it. However, it's gotten me nowhere closer to becoming friends with Porter the douchebag.

Zay's brows furrow. "How the hell is Raven supposed to help us with that?"

"Because she's good-looking enough, and Porter likes good-looking," Jax says in a bored tone, as if we're talking about the weather. "Plus, Raven isn't technically part of any family, so he won't be breaking any rules by getting close to her."

"*She's good-looking enough*," I mimic Jax's tone and roll my eyes. "She's fucking gorgeous, and you know it."

He stares at me without blinking, which might unnerve a lot of people, but I relax back in the chair.

Finally, Jax takes a seat in an empty chair. "Fine, she's gorgeous, but that only proves my point more. And we've been trying to get in with Porter for over a month. This way will be quicker and get us closer to our freedom, which is what we all want more than anything, right?" There's a challenge in his eyes as he looks at me, daring me to tell him that I've changed my plans about wanting to get the hell out of this town and away from this family mafia drama.

While I love challenging Jax, I won't with this. I've

wanted my freedom since the day we were brought into that mansion that Jax's dad lives in and shoved into that room with …

"Yeah, it's what we want," I agree with a heavy sigh. "But it feels kinda wrong using Raven… Honestly, I kind of felt that way last night when you suggested Zay play her. And Porter's a prick and likes women who are easy. And Raven's not easy. I don't think she's even experienced. So, I'm not sure your plan will work."

"Yeah, I don't think she's experienced either," Zay mutters, wiping his hand across his forehead.

I cast him an amused look. "You two should get along fantastically then."

He glowers at me. "Yeah right. She drives me crazy."

"I think you like that," I mock, eliciting another dirty look from him.

"Stop getting off track," Jax warns. "I need to make sure we're all on the same page about this. The last thing I need is one of you feeling guilty and backing out."

As he says it, that guilt I felt last night trickles through me again.

What is with this girl? Why is she getting under my skin so deeply?

"Why would we feel guilty?" Zay grumbles. "If she's gonna be part of our circle, she's gonna have to get used to doing stuff like this."

"Yeah, but we're kind of using her," I state the obvious, guilt pressing against my chest even harder. "Plus, we're digging up dirt on her for the bosses ..." I frown. "If she really was part of our circle, we'd be breaking a ton of rules."

"She's not part of our circle yet," Jax stresses. "And if we want to get the hell out of this life, both of these things need to be done. Technically, we don't have to use her to get to Porter, but we've been trying to get to him for a while and this is our best option. As for digging up dirt on her, that's non-negotiable. The bosses asked for it; so, we do it." He leans back and crosses his arms, his eyes looking a little bit bloodshot as he stares us down hard. "So, what's it going to be? Her or us?"

"Are those really the only two options?" I mumble with a frown.

"Unless you have a better idea, yes," Jax replies without an ounce of remorse in his expression.

Deep down, I wonder if he feels guilty. Usually, he doesn't. If Raven was just a normal girl, he wouldn't. But Raven isn't a normal girl. She's broken, just like all of us, which makes it so much worse when I hear Zay say, "Fine, I choose us."

They both look at me, waiting for me to choose, and while I hate myself for it, I know there's really only one choice. Because, in the end, I'll always choose Zay and Jax over anything.

I let out a sigh. "Fine, I choose us, too." Then I get up to leave the room to do a few more lines before school.

"There's one more thing," Jax calls out before I can leave.

I pull a face. Great. What the hell else is he gonna make us do?

I pause in the doorway and turn around. "What now?"

Jax's gaze bounces between Zay and me, and then he scratches the back of his neck. "A raven flies into the window this morning and for a brief second, my mind went to that dark place. It could be just a coincidence, but if it's not..."

The room grows quiet for a moment, all of us rippling with uneasiness.

"You really don't think they're gonna start that fucking game up again, do you?" I finally say, my voice shaky. "I mean, they'd tell us if they were... right?"

Jax says nothing, simply arching a brow. I know what he's thinking, though. That the bosses would definitely start up the game without telling us. In fact, they'd probably thrive on blindsided us with it.

And while I can't remember all of the detail of the game, a trait all of us share so I doubt it's coincidental, I know enough to understand that I don't want to play again.

"Relax," Jax says, sensing my tension. "We don't need to get worked up until we know for sure."

I nod, but inside, I remain worked up.

What if it happens again? What if our bosses force us to play again?

What if I hurt someone again?

3

RAVEN

THE FIRST TIME I REALIZED MY UNCLE BEN WAS A total nutjob was about a week after I moved in with him and my aunt. He had mostly ignored me up until then, although my aunt and cousin were pretty verbal about how much they loathed the new edition to their "perfect" family.

Before I moved in with them, I'd met my aunt, uncle, and cousin a whopping two times. Once was at my dad's parents' funeral after they died in a car crash. My uncle and my dad were the only children they had, which left them only having each other. According to my dad, though, he never got along with my uncle. He never embellished on the specifics, but I figured he wasn't a fan of my dad being a thief and a conman, since my uncle was —and is—a cop.

33

The second time my uncle made a presence in my life was a couple of weeks before my parents were killed. He just showed up at our house, something my mom was really upset about. I can't remember much about what happened while he was there, but my memory has always been pretty shitty. I can always remember having gaps in my memories; tiny holes that I could never fill.

I once asked my mom about it when I was younger and couldn't remember how I got home after school.

She felt my forehead for a fever then looked at me worriedly. "You don't feel warm, but maybe we should take you to a doctor just in case."

I shook my head. "No, I hate doctors."

She crouched down in front of me. "Now, Raven, remember what we talked about. Doctors help us. There's no reason to fear them."

I knew she was probably right. My mom usually was. But every time I even thought about going to see a man or woman wearing one of those creepy white coats, I felt like I was going to throw up—

"Raven! Are you up yet?" My aunt pounds on my shut bedroom door, startling me.

I've been awake since before the sun came up, ever since I woke up from that second dream then saw my uncle burning shit in the backyard. I haven't gotten up yet, though, partly because I've been overanalyzing the dreams and what the hell my uncle was burning, and partly because my side hurts like a bitch—

"Raven!" my aunt shouts again. "Wake up! You're taking the damn bus today, and it gets here in twenty minutes."

I grit my teeth but manage to say in an even tone, "Why can't I just ride with you when you drive Dixie May to school?"

"Dixie May's car arrived last night, so she's driving herself to school," she says. "You're taking the bus this morning. Dixie May doesn't need your moody, sullen, depressing presence ruining her chances of making friends here."

I scoot over to the edge of the bed. "Now, Auntie, I'm sure Dixie May's bitchy, slutty stupidity will make up for me cramping her style. In fact, I predict she'll have a minion of idiots following her around like mindless sheep by the end of the day." I stand up, wincing from the pain and tightness in my side.

"How dare you talk about my daughter like that?" She wiggles the doorknob and curses. "Open this door right now, Raven, or I swear to God—"

I throw open the door. "You'll what?"

She's standing on the other side, breathing furiously. Her blonde hair is pulled into a messy bun, and she's wearing a pair of yoga pants and a long-sleeved shirt, her usual morning look.

She takes a frustrated breath, her lips parting, her nostrils flaring. "You little shit—"

"Honey, remember what we talked about." My uncle appears in the hallway, dressed in his uniform, buttoning the top button of his shirt.

My thoughts go straight to what I saw last night, of him burning stuff in the darkness with people watching in the background. I still can't wrap my head around it. I mean, sure, my uncle is a creeper, but what I saw last night goes beyond the realms of weird.

"Right." My aunt's lips twist into a malicious grin as she looks at me. "The bus gets here in twenty minutes. If you miss it, you can walk." She tosses me a smirk then spins around and walks toward my uncle. When she reaches him, she places a kiss on his cheek, but he doesn't even so much as glance at her, his eyes fixed on me like a hawk.

Well, this is new. Usually, my uncle only acknowledges my presence when he's punishing me.

"Breakfast will be ready in ten minutes," my aunt tells him then whispers, "Last night was amazing." She gives him a lustful look then struts off toward the stairs.

I nearly vomit in my mouth at not only the idea of

them having sex but, if they were last night, then it might have been right after he …

I dry heave. Thankfully, I haven't eaten anything or I might have puked all over myself.

"Why are you looking at me like that?" My uncle approaches as he readjusts his belt.

I want to ask him what the hell he was burning in that fire last night and who was out there with him, but I know that'll get me nowhere, other than being pinned down by him on my bed again.

"I'm not looking at you." I step back into my room and move to shut the door.

He slams his hand against the door and holds it open. "You better start being more respectful toward me. I've got a whole list of words waiting to be carved into that pretty little flesh of yours."

So many words burn at the tip of my tongue, but I swallow them down, too tired and sore to get into it with him this morning.

"Yeah, that's what I thought." He grins, but a trace of disappointment reflects in his eyes. Still, he seems pretty damn chipper as he turns around and whistles as he walks away.

Flipping the middle finger at his back, I close the door. Then I grab a pillow, press it against my face, and scream. I scream until my lungs about burst. Until my chest aches.

I scream until I have nothing in me.

Then I lower the pillow from my face and sink down onto the bed, my gaze dropping to my scarred wrist.

Sometimes I think about doing it again—slicing open my wrist and trying to bleed the pain out. Maybe I will one day finally take that final step that will take me into an endless fall toward nothingness. It's what I thought was going to happen yesterday when I jumped off that bridge. But I didn't, and now I'm here, because Zay jumped in and pulled me out.

Part of me secretly hates him for doing it. For not just letting me keep falling forever. But he did, and now I'm here, walking around, feeling like I'm wobbling on the edge of a cliff that I could tip off of at any moment.

Fall, Raven. Just let yourself fall.

Maybe one day ...

Soon ...

Blowing out a breath, I drag my ass off the bed and start getting ready for school.

I decide on a black, short-sleeved shirt, with shorts, fishnet tights, and clunky boots. Then I put on a choker, my leather jacket, tie a plaid jacket around my waist, and call it good. I don't even bother doing my hair, just combing it to the side with my fingers. Then I dab on my usual minimal makeup—kohl eyeliner and lip gloss.

I go over to my computer chair where my bag always

is, but then I remember I left it at school.

Shit. I didn't even think about that until now. Just like I didn't think about how I have an absence for the last half of the day. I'm surprised my aunt didn't mention getting a call that I ditched school. Not that she cares. She just likes to make fun of me for being a loser and a "soon-to-be dropout."

But my aunt is the least of my problems. If this school works like my other, I'll get detention for the unexcused absence. So yeah, my day is going to be awesome.

I also don't have my iPod with me, so entering school is going to be an anxiety nightmare. It's my security blanket when people stare and whisper. And now I have to ride the bus ...

"Dammit, Zay, Jax, and Hunter," I grumble, even though I'm not sure that I'm really mad at them. Maybe I'm just irritated about my life. About the shittiness of it.

Feeling way too worked up, I decide to take a hit or two before I head out to the bus stop. Hopefully, that'll keep me chill long enough to get to my locker without panicking.

Grabbing a joint from my new secret spot—the inside of one of my old boots—I collect my lighter from the dresser drawer, lock my bedroom door, open the window, and then duck my head out. I pop the end of the joint between my lips, light up, and suck in a deep inhale.

Smoke laces in front of my face as I sit down on the windowsill, holding the joint outside while staring out at the scenery. The house I now call home is located in a small neighborhood of about ten houses, each spaced apart by at least five acres, so the chances of someone spotting me are pretty low. Just below my window is an inclined roof to the porch, and just in front of that is the dirt driveway lined with trees. Right beside it is the field where my uncle had his sketchy little bonfire party-of-one last night. In fact, I can still see remnants of the ash all over the ground.

It's driving me crazy that I don't know what he was doing out there.

I quickly become distracted when I spot a car cruising down the driveway, leaving a trail of dust in the air. And not just any car, but the prettiest Chevelle I've ever seen.

My dad used to be into cars. Up until he died, he drove a 1969 GTO Judge that was this really pretty light-blue color. This car is a similar shade but has a black hood. I'm not positive about the year, but I'd guess either a '68 or '69.

I watch as it pulls up to the house and parks next to my uncle's patrol vehicle. No one gets out right away, so I take another hit, waiting to see who the owner is. My bet is one of my uncle's new police buddies. Or maybe a neighbor. But then the passenger door opens and Jax climbs out.

No effing way.

I shake my head, sure I'm hallucinating. I glance at the joint. *Is this laced with something?* When I look back at the driveway, though, Jax is still there, standing beside the pretty as hell car.

He's dressed in a black shirt and matching jeans. Leather bands ornament his wrists, his facial piercing glint in the sunlight, and his inky black hair hangs in his eyes.

He doesn't notice me as he gazes at the lower section of the house. Then he turns toward the car, makes a signal with his fingers, and Hunter climbs out of the passenger side from the back seat.

He's wearing an all-black outfit, too, but his pants have pockets on the sides and a chain dangles from his beltloop. He's also sporting a short-sleeved shirt and has a knitted cap on his head, strands of his blond hair dangling out from it. Even from up here, he still looks too gorgeous to be real. Maybe he's not. Maybe none of this is. Maybe I really did die in the water yesterday and this is Hell.

Hell looks really good from up here.

I shake my head at my own stupid thoughts. Jesus, this thing must really be laced with something. That doesn't stop me from smoking some more.

I shift my gaze across them and to the driver's seat as I take another hit. The windows are too tinted to see inside, but I'm betting Zay is sitting there.

So they're here, in my driveway. But why—

Dixie May lets out a squeal from downstairs.

"Oh my God, Mom! You're never going to believe this!" She squeals again. "There are these guys that go to my school, and they're seriously, like, the hottest guys I've ever seen. Everyone wants to be with them, but they, like, never pay attention to anyone, though I talked to them for a little bit yesterday morning in first period. But anyway, they're outside in the driveway! Oh my God, I wonder if they're here to give me a ride to school or something. That'd be *amazing*!"

"Oh, honey, that *is* amazing!" My aunt sounds just as excited.

I'd be grinning over Dixie May's assumption that The Raven Three—Four—whatever they are, are here for her, but something she said has me frowning.

Jax, Hunter, and Zay talked to Dixie May yesterday morning? They never mentioned that.

I bring the joint to my lips to take another hit, letting the smoke hit my lungs and trying to smoke the worry out of me. What if everything that happened yesterday was some sort of elaborate prank Dixie May convinced the guys to do to me? Sure, The Raven Three don't seem like they'd be her sheep, but I've thought that before about people and been wrong.

I'm such an idiot.

"You want to rock, paper, scissors for it?" Hunter's voice floats up to me from down below.

Jax and him are now standing in front of the car, facing each other, their hands stuffed inside their pockets.

Jax cocks a brow at him. "That's your brilliant idea?"

Hunter shrugs, sitting down on the hood. "Unless you'll just let me go. But I have a feeling you're not gonna be down for that."

Jax sighs then sticks out his hand. So does Hunter.

Jax starts with the, "One, two, three—"

"Hey, guys." Dixie May steps off the porch and saunters down the walkway toward them. She has on high heels, a maroon dress, and her blonde hair is in a high, flawless ponytail, swishing as she walks.

As Jax and Hunter lower their hands to their sides and turn toward her, I look away, not wanting to see their reactions, not wanting to know the truth. Then I scrape the end of the joint against the side of the house to put it out, duck back inside, and shut the window.

Noting the time, I hide the joint back in my boot, spray some perfume on, and then head out of my room so I can go catch the bus.

And go live the pathetic life I deserve.

4

RAVEN

A few minutes later, I make it downstairs. The house is rather quiet, so I figure my uncle must've left for work already. But as I'm passing by the kitchen, I hear him murmuring to someone.

"No, I understand," he hisses. "I don't think the hypnosis is working, though... No, I've tried that... But... Look, I told you last night that it probably wouldn't work."

Hypnosis? Last night?

I pause near the doorway and lean against the wall, listening.

"Yeah, I guess I can try that, but... I don't know... Does doing drugs interfere with that sort of stuff? No, I have everything under control. That's not going to happen... I know it's been almost a decade, but that's the deal we made... if we want this to work... Yeah, I know it has to work or else we're fucked, but... Fine, send it out then and do a test," he says then I hear footsteps heading toward me.

Shit. I rush away, hightailing it away from there. But what he said fills my thoughts. Hypnosis? Drugs? Just who the hell is my uncle trying to hypnotize?

I think about what I saw last night and frown. I've always known my uncle was a shady dude, but this is an entirely new level of sketchy. But I may be able to use it to my benefit, if I can figure out what he's up to. Maybe this could be my ticket out of this house, if it's twisted enough and something I can prove to others. Then again, if I do leave this house, I'm unsure where I'd go since I have very little money and no form of transportation.

Sighing in frustration, I hurry toward the front door. As I pass the living room, I spot my aunt sitting on the sofa with her face pressed against the window, probably spying on Dixie May and the guys, like a creeper.

Dude, no wonder her and my uncle are married. They both like spying on people.

I stop near the doorway. "So, where's the bus stop?" I ask as I zip up my jacket.

"At the end of the driveway." She barely glances in my direction, a wistful smile pulling at her lips. "God, to be young again and have potential lovers showing up at your door. I miss it."

"I can't believe you still remember what it was like with how long it's been," I mumble, turning to leave.

"Oh, don't be so pissy, Ravenlee." She smirks at me. "Just because you're miserable, doesn't mean you need to hate the rest of us for being happy. Then again, I guess I can't really blame you. If I had to live your miserable existence, knowing no one will ever love you, I'd probably be miserable, too."

The muscles in my jaw pulsate as I turn toward the front door. "Your happiness is an illusion, Auntie," I call out as I open the door. "And one day, you'll realize that. Although, maybe not. You've never been one for seeing reality, even when it slaps you across your overly-injected Botox face."

"Why, you little shit—"

I hurry out the front door, knowing she won't chase me and risk making a scene.

Taking a deep breath, I shove all my feelings away and start down the walkway, attempting to appear as nonchalant as possible. My plan is to stroll right on by where Dixie May is prattling on animatedly to Jax and Hunter. Then I'll keep going until I reach the end of the driveway where the bus is supposed to pick me up. That's probably when my pride will break down; it's really hard to look chill when you're walking onto a long, banana-yellow vehicle that smells like feet and has a bunch of screaming kids on it. But I'm going to try my best.

Halfway down the walkway, though, my plan goes to shit when Hunter spots me, a huge smile breaking out across his face that confuses the crazy unicorns out of me.

"There's my new BFF." His gaze scrolls up and down me as he walks toward me with a bounce in his step—the dude is so bouncy. "I was just about to go lookin' for you. Thought you might try to ditch me or something because you forgot to make my bracelet last night." When he reaches me, he wraps his arms around me and hugs me as he spins me around in a circle.

The move shocks the hell out of me and makes the cuts on my side feel like they're getting torn open.

I tense, whimpering in pain, which makes him tense and pull back.

Worry creases his features. "What's wrong?"

"Nothing," I lie, gripping his shoulders stiffly.

Jax glances in our direction then walks away from Dixie May, heading toward us.

Dixie May gapes at him then at Hunter and me. "What the hell is actually happening right now?"

Strangely, the guys ignore her.

Hunter's concerned gaze burrows into me. "Little raven, I can tell you're in pain, so fess up. What happened?"

I tuck my arm protectively against my side. "It's not a big deal. I'm just a little sore from the stretches I did this morning." A lame response, but I think I'm a little stoned.

His gaze drops to my side then snaps back up. "Get in the car." The intensity in his tone throws me off. He's always been so happy and laidback until now.

"Hunter ..." I start, preparing a good protest.

"Now," Jax orders, striding toward us.

I give him a *really* look. "Dude, just 'cause you boss Zay and Hunter around, doesn't mean you can boss me around."

He gives me a tolerant look then snags ahold of my hand and pulls me out of Hunter's arms. Then he steers me toward the car, taking long, calculated strides. I have to shuffle to keep up with him.

Hunter trails behind us, muttering, "See what happens when you make big brother mad."

I narrow my eyes at him from over my shoulder.

He starts to smile but presses it back. "I refuse to be happy again until you tell us the truth," he tells me as Jax drags me past Dixie May.

Her jaw is practically hanging to her knees. "I don't understand ... What're you guys doing with her? This doesn't make any sense at all."

"Aw now, don't worry your little head, sweetheart,"

Hunter says, coming to a stop in front of her. "We'll take care of you eventually."

I glance back at Hunter with a *what the shit?* look.

He flicks a glance in my direction, his eyes sparkling with mischief. He's up to something, but what? Hopefully, it isn't trying to get into Dixie May's pants. I don't think I can be friends with him if he screws her. Then again, are these guys even trying to be my friend? That was kind of unclear last night.

What the hell is this thing between us?

Jax slows to a stop beside the passenger side of the car then releases my hand and turns back toward Hunter and Dixie May. He has a calculating look on his face, but I have no damn clue what he's calculating. Maybe he's just checking her out. Or maybe he's plotting the many ways he could torture her. Who the hell knows since his expression is so guarded?

While Jax may be interested in what Hunter is saying to Dixie May, I don't share the feeling. At least, that's what I try to convince myself. But then curiosity gets the best of me and I twist around to watch whatever the heck is about to happen.

Dixie May is smiling all doe-eyed at Hunter while raveling the end of her ponytail around her finger. "Really?" she asks, biting her bottom lip.

Hunter's eyes twinkle as he steps closer to her. "Yeah,

by the end of the week, you're going to feel completely taken care of." He traces a line down her cheekbone with his fingertip. "Do you want that? For me to take care of you?"

She flutters her eyelashes as she places her palm against his chest. "How about you just take care of me now? I can ride to school with you guys, and you can let my cousin ride the bus."

I love how she simply calls me cousin. If she wasn't trying to impress Hunter right now, I'd be freak or loser or murderer.

"Sorry, sweetheart, but little raven over there has gotta ride with us." He gives an innocent shrug. "It's part of the rules."

So that's why they picked me up—because it's a rule. Just how many rules are there? And what about this oath I'm supposed to take?

A crinkle forms between Dixie May's brows. "What rules?"

"You don't need to worry about that. In fact, you don't need to worry about anything, except me taking care of you." He gives her a toothy grin.

If yesterday had never happened, I'd just assume he was flirting with her. But his choice of words has me questioning exactly what Hunter has planned for Dixie May.

Is he threatening her in a subtle way? Or is he really just planning on screwing her?

Dixie May grins. "Okay. I'll see you at school then."

He nods, his gaze never wavering from hers. "Absolutely."

Hunter turns to walk away, but she grabs ahold of his arm. "Wait. Before you go, there's something you should know." She flicks a glance at me, a sly grin spreading across her face.

I roll my eyes, but her smirk only grows. Then she stands on her tiptoes, leans in toward Hunter's ear, and whispers something.

I don't have to hear the words to know what she's saying. It's the same thing she tells everyone when they show even a drop of interest in me.

Murderer.

Normally, this would be my cue to leave, but these guys already know about the blood staining my hands and they're still here. I'd question why, but I think I already know the answer.

Because they may be just as crazy as me.

"Really?" Hunter says as Dixie May steps back, sneaking a grin in my direction.

I try to get the upper hand by smiling and mouthing, *"your makeup case ..."* Then I draw my finger across my throat.

Her eyes widen as her lips part, but then her gaze skims across the guys and she collects herself, putting on her pretty, little, fake smile that I so often dream of cutting off.

"So, you should be careful around her," she says sweetly to Hunter.

He glances at me then back at her. "Thanks for telling me. I'll make sure to give her a thorough, *thorough* pat down before I get too close to her to make sure she's not packing any weapons." He winks at me, and I shake my head, trying really damn hard not to smile. But I'm fucking stoned, so I'm pretty sure a dopey-ass smile touches my lips.

Dixie May gives a confused, off-pitch laugh, her gaze shifting between Hunter and me. "Okay ... um ... good?"

With a grin, Hunter walks away from Dixie May and toward me and Jax. When he reaches me, he places his hand against the small of my back, turns me around, and urges me to get into the car. "You, little raven, get to ride in the back with me," he says cheerfully, skimming his finger along the sliver of flesh peeking out from between the hem of my shirt and the waistband of my shorts.

Jax rests an arm on top of the opened passenger door. "No, you're sitting up front," he tells Hunter. "I'll sit in the back seat with her."

Hunter shakes his head. "I sat in the back on the drive

here, so I get to continue sitting in the back if I want to."

Jax crooks a brow at him but doesn't utter a word. However, his intense gaze seems to convey some sort of silent message. That message goes way over my head, and part of me wonders if maybe I don't even want to know it. Don't want to know anything about what goes on inside these guys' minds. Then again, it probably isn't any worse than my own disturbing thoughts.

Finally, after what feels like an eternity, Hunter juts his bottom lip out. "Fine. Whatever, big brother." Then he steps back and gently nudges me toward the back seat.

I move to climb in, catching Dixie May's gaze. If looks could kill, I'd be a dead woman right now. Looks can't kill, though. No, Dixie May would have to have a weapon to follow through with that look. I would know since I used a knife to kill my parents. Although the knife was never found and was one of the reasons the police had such a hard time building a case against me. There was more to it than that, but truthfully, I've never fully looked into it. Never looked into the details of that awful day when I destroyed everything.

Freak.

Loser.

Unwanted.

Ugly.

Tainted.

Murderer.

Disappointment.

While I hate my uncle, the words he carved into my flesh fit me.

Instead of giving Dixie May a dirty look back, I lift my brow, challenging her to act upon that death look she's giving me.

Shaking her head, she spins around and stomps off toward the house.

I get a drop of satisfaction in for once. Although, it's not going to last—it never does. Soon, I'll be right back at the bottom of the totem pole, buried in the mud with the weight of everyone else pushing me down, burying me further, where I belong.

Buried in the ground, just like my parents.

Tearing my gaze off Dixie May, I start to climb into the car when my gaze lands on the field where the fire was last night.

My mom used to say that if I wanted to get to the bottom of the truth, I had to figure it out for myself. Of course, she usually said that when we were watching a mystery movie and I wanted to find out the ending without waiting for it. This isn't a movie, though. This is real life. But I still want answers, want to try to find a way to get the hell out of this house and this life, want to be free. Although, I'm not sure if I deserve it.

I chew on my bottom lip, deliberating. "Just a second," I say then swing around Jax and take off toward the field.

"Where are you going?" Hunter calls out after me.

"To look at something!" I shout back then move quickly even though my side hurts. I don't want my uncle to see me snooping around, so I have to move quickly.

A handful of seconds later, I reach the spot where the ashes are scattered. That's all that remains. Ashes. I don't know what I was expecting, but I'm disappointed. There aren't even any footprints in the dirt; no signs that people were out here. But I know they were. I saw it with my own eyes.

Unless I'm going crazy. Well, crazier than I already am.

What the hell happened last night?

I start to turn back around when something shiny and silver catches my eye. I crouch down, scoop it up, and my confusion doubles. It's a pendant shaped like a feather, and as the sunlight catches it, a dull pain sears in my mind.

Feathers ... floating around me ... I feel so at peace—

"Is everything okay?" Hunter's voice sails over my shoulder and mixes with the sound of approaching footsteps.

Clutching the pendant in my hand, I stand up and face him. "Yeah, my uncle was burning shit out here last night, and I wanted to see if I could figure out what it was. All I could find, though, was this." I show him the pendant.

He reaches out and touches the pendant. "Why would he burn this?"

"I'm not sure. I don't think it was the only thing he burnt, though. I just think the rest of it were papers."

"Your uncle do that kinda stuff often?"

"Yeah. He's a sketchy dude." A sketchy dude who likes to cut me all the time.

But I don't tell him that part.

No, I have no plans of telling anyone what happened to me last night.

Just like my uncle with this fire, I'm going to mentally burn that memory right out of my head.

"He also wasn't alone," I add. "There were people out here with him."

Hunter's brows knit. "What the hell? That's freakin' weird."

"I know," I agree, my gaze traveling to the spot on the field where I saw the silhouettes.

Who was out here last night? And why were they watching my uncle? Just what is he up to? If I can find out, I might be able to get the upper hand in this fucked-up mind game he's been playing with me for years.

5

RAVEN

Hunter doesn't say much during the short walk back to the car, which is a bit strange since, up until this point, he's seemed like a chatty sort of guy. He also appears slightly pale, as if he's sick. Maybe he is, but I don't ask him about it or his sudden quietness, since I'm being equally as quiet.

When we reach the car, Jax is on his phone, so I take the opportunity to slip by him and climb into the car. Zay is sitting in the driver's seat and, like yesterday, he has on a black hoodie with the hood pulled over the top of his head. His hands are resting on top of the steering wheel, so I can see that his knuckles are a bit scraped up. The wounds look fresh.

"Did you have another temper tantrum last night or

something?" I drag out my sassy attitude—my wall to protect myself—and greet him with a smirk.

He looks at me, a grin curling at his lips as he lifts one of his hands from the steering wheel. "You talking about these, princess?"

Great, we're still on that whole princess nickname thing.

My eyes instantly travel to the scar on his jawline, just like the boy had in my dream. I wait for some sort of recognition to click, a sign that maybe it was a memory and not a dream, but not even a flicker of familiarity sparks from inside my brain.

What is wrong with me? Has my head finally just broke? Or do I know him? If so, does he remember me? I should ask him—I should—but a faint memory flickers at the back of my mind, one I'd almost forgotten about ...

"Whatever happens, Ravenlee, don't trust anyone," my dad tells me. "Promise me you won't. Promise me you'll always keep your guard up. Who you are ... it's dangerous if anyone finds out."

"You okay?" Zay stares at me like I'm a crazy person who's about to go off the deep end.

I smash my lips together, desperately fighting back the urge to just ask, *Do we know each other?*

"I'm just peachy," I manage to say in an even tone. Then I shove away the pain inside my head and scoot forward in the seat, changing the subject away from me. "Now it's your turn."

He stares at me, completely puzzled. It's kind of a cute look for him, which is an interesting combination with how scary he looks. "For what?" he asks.

"To tell me what happened to your hands. Because I'm pretty sure you didn't have those cuts when I left the house last night."

"I didn't." His lips twist into a dark smile as he leans closer to me. "I spent the night using a liar's face as my own personal punching bag."

I eye him over. "Are you being serious or just messing with me?"

"Does it look like I'm being serious?" he asks with an arch of his brow.

"Yeah, but you always look that way. In fact, I think serious is all you can do with that intense face of yours. Well, that and glaring. You're really good at that."

Zay sears me a nasty look while Hunter lowers his head inside the cab to look at us, strands of his hair falling across his forehead.

"Dude, my BFF is so awesome and, like, super clever," he muses with a smile, the paleness in his face no longer present.

I guess he got over whatever the heck was bothering him.

Behind him, Jax wanders off down the driveway, his boots scuffing against the dirt as he talks on his phone. He speaks too quietly for me to hear what he's saying, and his face is a blank canvas, so I can't even attempt to read him. Although, I doubt I could anyway.

Zay rotates forward in the seat again and mumbles, "Quit calling her your BFF."

"Why?" Hunter asks with a twinkle in his eyes. "That's what she is."

"No, she's not." Zay pierces him a firm look.

Hunter keeps on grinning, but I swear I detect the slightest falter in his almost constant happiness.

"There are no rules against me being BFFs with our little raven," he declares.

"Dude, you guys really need to stop calling me yours," I interrupt with an eye roll.

Hunter casts a playful grin in my direction then looks back at Zay. "It's so cute that she actually believes she isn't ours now."

Zay thrums his fingers against the top of the steering wheel, seeming worked up about who the hell knows what. "She needs to quit being ridiculous. She jumped; therefore, she belongs to us now, whether she likes it or not... whether we like it or not."

"I don't belong to anyone." I cross my arms. "And that's not a ridiculous thing to say. It's not normal to belong to someone, especially when you don't even want them to belong to you."

Hunter looks at me like he finds me absolutely entertaining. "First of all, we do want you to belong to us. Zay is just full of shit. And second, when you're in our circle, you will belong to us."

I start to tell him that I'm not technically in their circle, but Hunter cuts me off.

"You'll officially be in it today after you take the oath." The edges of his lips curve upward. "And then you'll belong to us, and we'll belong to you. That's how it works, little raven."

"Then, doesn't that mean you guys belong to each other, too?" I question with a snarky grin, figuring that'll get them to stop, that these tough-ass guys won't want me saying they belong to each other.

But Zay says nothing, while Hunter merely shrugs.

"Yeah," he says, unbothered.

Well, okay then ...

I rack my mind for a better comeback but come up blank.

Damn, I really need to start eating breakfast and drinking coffee in the morning to wake myself the hell up. The problem is, nine times out of ten, my uncle is in the kitchen, and I'd rather starve and be deprived of caffeine than willingly go into a room that he's in.

"It's part of the rules," Hunter adds with an adorable lopsided grin. "That we belong to each other."

"What other rules are there?" I ask, recalling how they mentioned rules several times yesterday, yet only one was specified.

"A lot of other stupid ones," Hunter sulks but then wavers. "Well, not all of them are stupid. But the new ones Jax made up last night are."

"Do I get to know these rules?" I shift in the seat. "Or are you guys gonna just keep on tiptoeing around them?"

"Yeah, you get to know them." Jax appears by the open door. He nudges Hunter out of the way, ducks his head into the car, and then slides into the seat beside me. "Because you're going to follow them, too."

My brow teases upward. "I don't remember ever agreeing to that."

He reclines in the seat. "Being in this car means you're agreeing to it. It also means you've agreed to be in our circle." He says it like that's that and there's no arguing. Apparently, he's never been around a girl like me before.

I rotate in the seat toward him. "I never asked you guys to pick me up this morning."

He stares at me without a drop of emotion in his eyes, which makes his gaze unnerving. I refuse to look away, though, even though he's making me feel kind of squirrely.

He might be the hardest person to read ever.

"You know what? You're right." With his gaze welded to mine, he slams his hand against the back of the seat right as Hunter is leaning it back. Then he shoves it forward.

"What the hell, Jax?" Hunter gapes at him as he jumps back out of the car.

Jax's gaze remains welded to mine. "I think it stops at the end of the driveway. Am I right, Zay?"

"I'm not sure." Zay picks up his phone from off the middle of the seat. "I can look it up."

I know I should just drop it and be grateful that I don't have to ride the bus, but their bossiness drags the stubbornness out of me. I might really be a freak 'cause part of me kind of gets off on this.

"You don't need to look it up, Zay. I know where the bus stop is." I keep my gaze on Jax as I signal for him to move out of my way with a flick of my wrist. "Let me out. I've got a bus to catch."

"Stubborn fucking girl," Zay mutters, tossing his phone onto the seat beside him.

Jax stares at me for a beat. "Fine. If you want to get out, then get out. No one's stopping you." A challenge glints in his eyes as he remains where he is and crosses his arms.

And I desperately want to win that challenge. I'm not

even sure why, other than I hate being bossed around. It's become my life, and I'm getting so tired of it. Tired of being controlled. So, lifting my chin defiantly, I kneel up on the seat, turn around, and swing my leg over his lap to climb over him. When I smack my head on the roof, I grimace.

Smooth, Raven. Really smooth.

But I keep going, moving farther over Jax's lap.

Hunter watches the scene from outside the car with sparkling curiosity. "What're you doing?"

"Getting out of the car." I shift my weight forward but end up smacking my head on the roof again. "Dammit." I sink down on Jax's lap and rub my head.

As my ass touches Jax's lap, he takes a sharp inhale of breath and clamps his hands down on my sides. It might be the first kinda, sorta emotion I've seen from him. Although, I'm not sure what it is. Surprise? Shock?

I may have tried to decipher it, but when he wraps one of his hands around my fresh, new wound, I suck in a shallow breath and clutch the back of the seat as pain scorches through my side.

Jax loosens his grip on me and slides his hands down to my hip instead. Then he picks me up and deposits me back onto the seat beside him.

"Get in the car," he orders Hunter. "Now."

Hunter's gaze bounces between Jax and me. "Sure

thing, big brother." He appears a bit confused as he moves to get into the passenger seat.

"No, Hunter, don't get in," I try to sound as demanding as Jax. "I need to get out first. The bus is gonna be here soon." I push past the pain and slide toward Jax again.

He snaps his arm out in front of me, barricading my way out. "You're not going anywhere until you tell us what happened to your side."

"Nah, I'd rather not." I flick my wrist at him. "Now, come on; move out of my way so I can get out and you guys can go back to only belonging to each other."

He stares at me, unimpressed. Then he slants forward, blocking my way even more, that challenge reflecting in his eyes again.

I scoot closer to him, pressing my knee into the side of his thigh. Still, he doesn't budge, so I inch closer until my leg is practically on his lap.

"For the love of God," Zay groans in frustration, bobbing his head back. "Will one of you just give up?"

When neither Jax nor I move away from one another, Zay grumbles a few choice words then rotates around in the seat, his gaze landing on me. "Princess, just let this go or we're gonna be here all damn day. Jax is a stubborn bastard. Even worse than me."

"You're not that bad," I inform Zay, keeping my gaze

fixed on Jax. "In fact, the last time I tried to challenge you, it worked in my favor."

"How do you figure?" he asks, sounding perplexed.

My lips quirk as I flick a glance in his direction. " 'Cause I'm the one who sat in *your* seat during class, didn't I?"

The muscle in Zay's jaw pulsates, and Hunter chuckles under his breath, while Jax presses his pierced lips together. If I didn't know any better, I'd guess he was struggling not to smile. But, at this point, I'm catching on that he might never smile or react with any other emotion besides demanding indifference, if that even makes any sense.

"You didn't win that challenge," Zay argues, sliding his arm across the back seat. "I won it when you jumped off the bridge."

I lift my brow. "I thought you said you guys didn't really want me to jump? That you were just trying to scare me?"

He leans closer to me, his eyes darkening. "We didn't want you to jump, but you did, and now you belong to us ..." His lips kick up into a smirk. "So, who really won?"

"I don't. Belong. To you," I stress. For reals, though, how many times do I have to say this before they understand? "And even if I did, I wouldn't necessarily consider that winning."

A smirk pulls at his lips. "You're right. You're way too much of a pain in the ass to be a reward."

"Exactly. So how about you guys let me out of the car and we can forget yesterday happened?" Deep down, though, in a place I didn't even know existed, I feel this weird, raveling sensation, like my stomach is winding into knots.

"You're not going anywhere," Jax says, "so stop arguing." I start to retort when he places a finger over my lips, something he also did to me yesterday. "Stop. Arguing." He gives me a stern look before lowering his finger and slanting back in the seat. Again, he doesn't give me any time to protest, moving right along to his next order. "Now, here's what's going to happen. You're going to tell us what happened to your side. Then, when that's done and handled, we'll go over the rules with you so that you know what you can and can't do. And there won't be any more arguing."

"I'm not a fan of rules. And I'm not really big on telling other people my personal shit," I say, again thinking of that damn doctor I suddenly keep remembering. From what I can recall, he knew more about me than anyone else did, besides my parents. And what did he do to me? Well, from what little I can remember ...

For some reason, my fingers drift to my pocket where the feather pendant is. I brush my fingertips along the metal and get the strangest sense of peace again.

WTF?

What is this thing?

"How about I just go get on that bus?" I say, figuring it might be for the better if I take a break from these guys and try to clear my head and try to figure out what the hell this pendant is. "And you guys can go on with your lives, bossing other people around who will actually listen. Like Dixie May. She'll probably be more than happy to listen to you guys."

"Oh, I have big plans for your cousin," Hunter assures me as he sits down in the front seat and twists around to look at me with a devious grin spreading across his face. "Big, fun, wild plans."

"Good for you," I say. "If you want to fuck her, go ahead. Just don't give me a recap. You should probably wrap it up, though. She gets around."

Hunter stares at me for a blink then busts up laughing. "You think I'm going to fuck your cousin?" He points back at the house. "Her? Seriously?"

I shrug. "I don't know why you're acting like that's shocking. Dixie May may be a lot of things, but she's also gorgeous and flirty, and some guys apparently like that ... She's had a lot of boyfriends."

Hunter rubs his hand across his mouth, I think to

conceal a smile. Then he trades a glance with Zay, who gives him a wide-eyed, pressing look. Jax doesn't remove his gaze from mine, but a pucker forms at his brows.

"What?" I ask defensively. "Why're you guys looking at me like I'm crazy?"

Because you are, Raven.

A crazy freak.

Hunter trades another look with Zay then looks at Jax. "Can I answer this one, or are you going to? Because I'm not going to play the silent game with this. She needs to understand."

Jax is a mask of control as he assesses me. "Yeah, I guess you can. Just make sure you choose your words carefully." He gives Hunter a warning look then reclines against the seat.

Giving Jax a salute, Hunter shuts the door then everyone grows quiet.

"You guys are weird," I state the obvious. "Is this how you usually act?"

Zay snorts a laugh. "Fuck no. That's all you, princess." He glances at me from over his shoulder. "Your stubbornness and inability to cooperate has us all messed up in the head."

"Sorry," I say unapologetically. "If I'm that annoying, you should just let me get on the bus."

He grips the wheel and shoves the shifter into reverse.

"It's not annoying. It's just ..." He trails off, backing the car up and turning it around.

Again, I'm left confused, which seems to be a reoccurring theme whenever I'm around them.

Silence skips by as Zay drives toward the end of the driveway.

Halfway down, Hunter looks at me again with a contemplative look on his face. "You wanna know why some guys want your cousin?" he asks. "And I mean, the real reason. Not your naïve assumption."

"Hey, I may be a lot of things, but I'm not naïve," I protest. "I've seen a lot of dark shit in my time. Like, way more than your average person."

"Oh, I don't doubt that," he agrees, crossing his arms on the back of the seat. "But I'm not talking about dark shit. I'm talking about sex, something I'm starting to wonder if you know anything about."

I roll my eyes. "Again, I'm not a naïve idiot. I know what goes where and how to get it done."

An amused smile plays at the corners of his lips. "Yeah, but have you ever had the what in your where? Or, in less naïve terms, a dick in your pussy."

Zay shakes his head as he steers the car out of the driveway and onto the highway that leads to the main part of town. "What the hell, Hunter?" he mumbles.

"Careful," Jax warns Hunter with an icy look. "Don't cross that line."

Hunter tries to charm him over with a dazzling smile. "Chill, big brother. I got this."

Zay mumbles something under his breath again, and Jax presses Hunter with another cold look.

"I hope you do," he warns.

Hunter just grins then looks at me. He assesses me with a spark of mischievousness in his eyes. "Have you?" he finally asks.

I get the feeling he's trying to embarrass me, and he kind of is, but I'm not about to allow him to have the satisfaction of knowing that. So, I dig out my façade of indifference. "Have I had a cock in my pussy?" I ask, carrying his gaze.

Delighted surprise flickers in his eyes. "Yeah, little raven, that's what I'm eagerly waiting to hear the answer to."

"Why does it matter?" I question.

He lifts a shoulder. "For a couple of reasons. One being so I can figure out how I want to explain this whole Dixie May situation that you've gotten all wrong."

"I'm not wrong about guys wanting her," I insist. When none of them make any effort to say anything, I let out a loud sigh. "Fine. You want me to say it, then I'll say. Yeah, I'm a virgin. No one's put their cock in my pussy.

No one's really touched me. No one's ever kissed me ... Well, sort of ..." Memories try to pierce inside my mind, but I stifle them. "But, so what? There are plenty of virgins walking around in this world. I'm *not* an anomaly."

No one says anything right away, as if I've shocked them all into silence. Even Hunter, which seems almost impossible.

Finally, Zay clears his throat and shifts. That seems to draw everyone out of their stupor spell that my stupid mouth seemed to cast over them.

Hunter eyes me over curiously. "So weird."

"What is?" I ask, giving him a yeah-I'm-the-weird-one look.

He shakes his heads, still looking at me the same way. "I'm just wondering how."

"How what?" I brace myself for whatever's coming. I can tell something bad is about to happen.

He wets his lips with his tongue, a strange look of curiosity flashing across his expression. "How you're a virgin." He shakes his head. "Fuck, how have you not even been kissed before?"

"Actually, she said she *sort of* hasn't been kissed," Zay says, his gaze straying to the rearview mirror and colliding with mine. "She never explained what that meant."

"And I'm not going to," I reply. "So, can we please just stop talking about this?"

Wisps of Hunter's blond hair fall into his eyes as his gaze sweeps across my body. Then he sinks his teeth into his bottom lip and looks me in the eye. "Nah, I wanna keep talking about it or else it's gonna be on my mind all damn day."

"Hunter ..." Jax cautions. "Rule number one."

Hunter scrunches his nose. "Dammit, Jax, you're always ruining my fun." He sighs when Jax continues to stare him down. "Whatever. I'll back off ..." He momentarily frowns then fixes a smile onto his face as he looks at me again. "Guys like screwing your cousin, little raven, not because she's some gorgeous goddess but because she's probably an easy lay."

"Maybe that's true, but she's still pretty," I tell him with a shrug. "Tons of people have said so. And even though I don't like her and think she's totally vile, she is pretty. That's something that just is what it is. And while I get that not every guy is into looks, there were a huge handful of them at our old school who were, and so Dixie May had quite the little groupie fan base that basically did whatever she asked."

And her favorite thing to ask was for them to torment me.

Hunter crinkles his nose. "She's okay-looking, but she tries to look that way. And whatever. If she wants to look good, then go ahead. It's not really the point of this conversation." He angles his head to the side as he reaches over the seat and sweeps his knuckles across my cheek. "Have you actually looked at yourself in a mirror? Or does your aunt and uncle not give you that privilege either?"

I lean away from his touch, feeling all sorts of weird about it.

I've spent so long not being touched until these guys entered my life twenty-four hours ago. And while I may not hate it, skin-to-skin contact makes me feel way out of my element.

"Yeah, I've looked in a mirror. My life isn't that crazy. But I don't look in it that much because I don't try to look pretty." I also hate seeing the scars all over my body, but I'm not going to tell them that. "And I don't really care if am."

"I'm also not blind. I know my cousin is pretty. And from past experiences, her looks have gotten her what she's wanted a lot. And right now, she wants you guys."

"I'm sure you're right. And I never said she wasn't pretty, just that it wasn't a completely natural pretty. I also said that wasn't the point I was trying to get across." Hunter reaches for me again. "Have you ever really looked at yourself? And I mean *really* looked at yourself without thinking about all the shit people have said to you?" He grazes the pad of his thumb along my bottom lip. "Have you ever paid attention to your lips? Have you ever tried to bite on them to get your way?" He then sketches his fingertip underneath my eye. "And those eyes. All you'd have to do is bat them at someone and you could get whatever you want. You just didn't know any of this, so you haven't done it." He lowers his hand from my face. "And don't even get me started on the rest of you." His gaze deliberately scans up and down my body.

I crinkle my nose, hoping he'll stop talking because it's making me extremely uncomfortable. I can't recall the last time anyone said anything nice to me—probably when my parents were alive—so I feel like Hunter is about to start laughing in my face and tell me he's joking.

"Those long legs and that fucking ass ..." He sinks his teeth into his bottom lip. "It was the first thing I saw yesterday morning when I walked into the office. And fuck, if it wasn't the best way to start my day. It was almost as good as getting fucked. Although, probably not as good as actually fucking you in the—"

"All right, that's enough," Jax cuts him off, his gaze searing into Hunter.

I attempt to appear calm on the outside. Inside, I'm a mess. The compliments ... the things he said ... no one has ever spoken to me that way before, and I don't know whether to be wary, appalled, or turned on. My body doesn't seem to know either as a shiver rolls through me.

Luckily, I'm a pro at keeping my cool and manage to act indifferent.

Hunter, though, looks all sorts of worked up, his gaze blazing. But then he blinks, as if coming out of some sort of daze, and shifts his gaze to Jax. Surprisingly, he glares at him. "No, it's not. She needs to hear this. Her confidence is so damn low it's ridiculous."

"Hey, I can hear you," I say, but they ignore me.

"And I told you to be careful with your choice of words," Jax tells Hunter in a low tone. "You're about to cross a line, and I'm sure you know you are. You're getting too worked up, so take a timeout, turn around, and focus on something else besides her."

Hunter smashes his lips together, his gaze flitting from me to Jax. "Fine." He turns around, crosses his arms, and stares out the window, pouting.

Silence settles amongst the four of us. Jax is clearly annoyed. So is Hunter. Zay ... I can't see his face, but his knuckles are white as he grips the wheel.

Awesome. I've caused a fight between them already.

See? This is why you don't have friends.

I start to suggest that maybe they should take me home, though the bus has probably come and gone by now, but then Jax turns to me.

"Now, why the hell does your side hurt this morning?" he asks, or more like demands.

I startle a bit from his abrupt shift in topic, but then I recover and shake my head. "I already said—"

He puts that damn finger against my lips again. "Either you're going to tell me, or I'm going to lift your shirt and see for myself."

I narrow my eyes at him. "Go ahead. I'll fight you—you know I will. But what you don't know about me is that I've got a wicked right hook. I just didn't get a chance to use it yesterday. Today, I'm more prepared."

"I'm sure you are," he says without an ounce of emotion in his tone. "But trust *me*; I'll win this fight. I always do, because I always do whatever it takes to win."

"So do I," I lie haughtily. Then I lift my chin, refusing to look weak.

Jax's eyes shadow over, his pierced lips parting. "If you think—"

"Zay, pull the car over for a minute," Hunter announces abruptly.

Jax's gaze cuts to Hunter. "Why?" he asks at the same time Zay gives him a confused look and mutters, "Wait ... You're not ...?"

Hunter gives Zay an indecipherable look then looks at Jax. "I know you think I can't handle this, but just let me talk to her privately for, like, five minutes. You guys can keep an eye on me from the car, and if it looks like I'm getting out of control, tape my mouth shut and make me ride in the trunk." His lips quirk with amusement. But underneath the humor, I detect the slightest bit of sadness reflecting in his eyes.

I wonder what it is, what could possibly make the most upbeat guy I've ever met sad.

Jax meticulously studies him. "Are you going to …?"

Hunter swallows hard then nods. "Yeah … I think it might help. With *everything*."

Jax considers what he said then nods. "We'll give you five minutes. That's it, though. And keep on topic. No straying off to her ass or legs, got it?"

Hunter nods.

Sighing, Zay slows the car down and steers it over onto a flattened space on the side of the road near a cluster of trees. An old farmhouse is in the distance, but other than that, nothing else is around, so there are no witnesses if they decide to pull a stunt like they did yesterday.

"You do realize I can hear you guys, right?" I say, my lips moving against Jax's finger since he hasn't pulled it away yet.

"Really?" Hunter mockingly gasps. "This whole time I thought you were deaf. Crap, I hope I didn't say anything offensive." He pulls a *whoopsie* face.

I blast him a *hardy har har* look, to which he responds with a cheeky grin.

Jax lowers his finger from my lips then pats the back

of Hunter's seat. "Hurry up. I want to have time to go over the rules with her."

Hunter gives him a salute then pushes the door open, hops out, and lifts the seat up. Then Jax lowers his head and climbs outside, too. A couple of seconds tick by where they simply stand there before Hunter glances back into the cab, strands of his hair hanging in his eyes.

"Come on, little bird; you and I need to talk about a few things," he tells me, weirdly without grinning.

"Little bird," the doctor whispers in my ear, causing goosebumps to sprout across my flesh. "Close your eyes ..."

"Fine." I grimace as I cross the seat toward him. "But please don't call me little bird. If you have to call me something other than my name, then just stick with little raven, okay?"

A crease forms between his brows, but he nods. "Okay. Little raven it is."

I appreciate his lack of arguing about this and offer him a small smile. "Thanks."

He smiles back and mutters, "So fucking beautiful."

Luckily, Jax doesn't hear him, or else I think he would have chewed his ass out. Me? I roll my eyes so damn hard they nearly get stuck in the back of my head.

But all Hunter does is give me an innocent look. "What? I'm just stating the truth."

Rolling my eyes again, I move to climb out, and

halfway out, Hunter takes my hand, unnecessarily helping me the rest of the way. When I'm standing, he doesn't release my hand, guiding me past Jax and toward some trees.

My guard immediately goes up, and I curl my free hand into a fist, preparing to fight if I need to. "Where are we going?"

"Into those trees," Hunter replies as he continues to pull me forward, his clunky boots scuffing the dirt. "I need some privacy for this."

My stomach ravels into knots again, but this time it's an unpleasant sensation.

Maybe I am naïve, I realize. I mean, I got in a car with these guys without a phone or anything, and now I'm wandering into the trees with one of them.

I have a feeling something bad is about to happen.

The worst part is, I did it to myself.

6

RAVEN

Unnerving silence stretches between us as Hunter leads me closer to the trees and farther away from civilization.

"Relax." He gives my hand a squeeze. "None of us are ever going to hurt you."

"I'm not worried about you hurting me," I lie coolly. I kind of am, but I'm not going to freak out. It's not my style. No, I'm going to remain calm until I need to fight.

Once tree branches and shade surround Hunter and me, he comes to a stop and faces me. He parts his lips, but then he startles as birds scatter from the trees, leaving feathers floating in the air.

Flap...

Flap...

Flap...

I blink as shadows of memories start to tug at my mind. What the hell was that?

I glance at Hunter and he blinks too, then looks at me with this brows puckered.

"Okay…" He seems distracted. "I think this should be good enough."

I feel as equally as distracted. Why did I feel like I was about to fly away with those birds? Talk about crazy. "Good enough for what?"

"For it to just be you and me." He threads his fingers through mine again and smiles at me, but it doesn't quite reach his eyes. "I know it's hard to trust people. Trust me; I get that—we all do. But we're never going to even get a chance to earn your trust if you won't trust us even a little. In order to gain trust, you have to give trust a little bit, if that makes any sense."

"Yeah, it does, but that doesn't mean I can just give it." I give a half-shrug. "It's almost instinctive for me to not trust people." For a lot of reasons.

In fact, I don't even trust myself, which is a little weird, but seriously, how can I when my mind has literally erased itself a handful of times. I'm like a computer that likes to occasionally crash.

"And again, I understand that, so I'm gonna attempt to put a little fracture in your instinct by trusting you enough to show you something that no one except for Zay,

Jax, and the person who did this to me knows about." He opens and flexes his free hand and takes an uneven breath.

He's nervous.

Why's he nervous?

When he lifts up the hem of his shirt, I have my answer.

Long, thin, but deep scars cover his sides, chest, and waist.

"What happened?" I ask, glancing up to meet his gaze.

He lowers his shirt, then a breath trembles from his lips. "My dad had this mistress ... She was bad ... even worse than my real mom ..." His hand starts to tremble in mine, so he pulls away and crosses his arms, tucking his hands underneath his armpits. "But anyway, she's a bitch who gets off on using her power on people who are weaker than her. And when I was younger, I was a lot weaker than her ... And, well, she used to do things to me a lot ... And she would scratch me a lot while she did those things to me."

He doesn't specify what the *things* are, but with the way he's trembling, I get a pretty good idea.

I'm not really certain what to say to him. I've never had anyone confide in me with something so personal. It makes me feel uncomfortable; enough that I just want to get back in the car. But he's also standing here in front of me, shivering from what I'm fairly sure isn't the cold, and the sight of it tugs at a memory of me trembling in a bed while my uncle leaned over me and carved the word *freak* into my side. It was the first time he did it, and I was freakin' terrified. But I learned quickly to numb myself.

"I'm sorry," I finally say. Then, before I can back out, I reach for the hem of my own shirt and lift it up, putting all my scars and the fresh wounds on display for him.

As soon as the chilly air hits my skin, a shiver courses through my body. At least, that's what I tell myself. Deep down, though, I know the cold air isn't what has my body quivering.

Fear. There it is again. And I really don't like it.

I start to tug my shirt back down when he captures my hand.

"Jesus," he whispers, reaching out and tentatively touching my skin. He starts at the top, tracing each letter marking my flesh with his fingertips, slowly working his way to the bottom. When he reaches the fresh wound, he pauses, his gaze traveling up to mine. "He did this to you last night?" he asks, his gaze searing into mine.

"I never said it was a he," I reply coolly, my guard going back up.

He gives me a tolerant look. "You may have not said the words aloud, but we know your uncle did this to you."

He strokes my cheek with his knuckles. "It's okay to say it aloud. Whatever he threatened you with to keep you silent, we won't let him do to you. We won't let him hurt you."

"He didn't threaten me with anything." Which is the truth. "I just know that no one's gonna believe me." With him being a cop and me being a once accused killer, that's the real truth.

He dips his head, leveling his gaze with mine; his expression soft, cautious. "I'll believe you. I promise I will."

"Because of the rules?" I question with cynicism.

"No, because I know that ugly exists in this world and that people who are supposed to love and take care of us end up being the worst tormentors."

His words strike a nerve inside me, but I can't get the words—the truth I've been carrying inside me for years—to leave my lips.

"Hunter ... I ..." I trail off as he cups my face between his hands.

"Just trust me, like I trust you," he says, his gaze searing into mine.

Trust. What the hell is it even? I have no plans of finding out, but he just keeps on staring at me, waiting, and waiting, and waiting.

"Trusting people is hard," I finally confess.

"I know," he agrees. "But sometimes, when the person is trustworthy, it can feel really fucking good to trust them." For a brief moment, guilt flickers in his eyes, but it happens so swiftly that I wonder if I imagined it.

"I wouldn't know," I mutter, feeling so damn tired.

Of fighting. Of everything.

When I look back at this moment, I won't be able to say why I decided to confide in someone. But something definitely changes in me the second I utter the words aloud. Whether it's a good change or a bad one, I haven't got a damn clue.

"I came home from you guys' place, and my uncle had found out I've been stealing from his drug stash," I start, feeling terrified, a completely new feeling for me, which seems crazy considering I jumped off a bridge yesterday. But that seemed easy in comparison to trusting someone. Trust is fucking scary. "He pinned me down on the bed and carved that"—I gesture at the word *disappointment* —"into my side."

Frowning, he gently touches the scars again. "Why didn't you call us? Didn't Zee give you the card?"

"Yeah, but I didn't have my phone, remember? And we don't have a house phone."

He frowns. "Shit. I didn't even think about that. I'm so damn sorry, little raven. I really am ... I'm going to make it up to you somehow."

"You don't need to do that. Honestly, I probably wouldn't have called you anyway."

"You should always call us when you need help," he insists in what I'm assuming is a stern tone for him, but it's filled with too much gentleness. "In fact, promise me you will."

"I can't promise that."

"Then we're gonna stand here all damn day."

"Fine, I promise." It's a total lie.

Asking for help ... trusting people ... it's not my thing.

He looks down at my scars. "Did he put all of these on you?" He doesn't remove his hand, keeping it on my scars just underneath my shirt.

"Yeah, he started doing it years ago. He does it when I do something that really pisses him off. Although, he's been doing it more frequently the older I get. But that might be because I get in more trouble now than I used to." I sink my teeth into my bottom lip, wavering. "I don't know. He kinda seems to ... get off on it, so maybe he just likes doing it."

His brows furrow, his eyes crinkling at the corners as sunlight hits him directly in the face. "What do you mean by that exactly?"

"That he seems to like doing it to me." I shrug as the wind blows wisps of my hair into my eyes. "I think, right after he cut me last night, he went and had sex with my aunt, so ... yeah ..." I shrug again.

He sucks in a shaky breath through his nose then gradually releases it. "I think we need to get you out of that house."

I blink at him. "What?"

He skims his knuckles across my cheekbone. "You need to move out of your aunt and uncle's house. In fact, I think it's extremely important that you do." He dazes off a bit, seeming in pain.

"As appealing as moving out sounds, it's not gonna happen. At least not until I'm eighteen. Even then, my uncle will put up a fuss if what Zay said yesterday is true, about my uncle getting money for taking care of me when I graduate." No, the only way I'll ever get out of that house before I graduate is if I can find something to basically blackmail my uncle with. "Plus, I've got, like, a total of a hundred bucks to my name. That's not enough to rent an apartment. I could try to steal some from my aunt and uncle, but they don't keep a lot of cash in the house. And getting a job is a pain in the ass since I have no car, don't know how to drive, and there's no real bus system in this town."

"We can take care of all that," he assures. "Jax has already been calculating a way for us to take care of your uncle like we promised. But this way we can take care of two problems at once. Your uncle loses his money, and you get to move out of that house. It's a win, win." He gives a short pause, his gaze dropping fleetingly to my side again. "Not that we're not gonna make him hurt. We're gonna make sure that asshole more than understands the pain he put you in." A dark smile turns upward at his lips. "You can even help us if you want."

"You want me to help you hurt my uncle?" I question. "For reals?"

He nods, tucking a strand of hair behind my ear. "You wanna do that? Hurt him like he hurt you?"

God, do I want to. But I'm also bit apprehensive over the idea, wondering if I unleash that kind of darkness inside me, will I end up killing someone?

"You don't have to help us if you don't want to," Hunter adds when he notes my hesitancy.

"No ... I want to. I'm just wondering how you guys plan on doing that without getting arrested. And, how are you going to help me move out of the house? Because, like I said, I have no money and no real way to earn money, so I can't afford my own place. Unless you guys wanna be my own personal taxi and drive my ass to work and back."

"It won't be that difficult making your uncle pay. We just gotta be calculating and careful about it. Jax is really good at that shit, so I know he'll figure something out. Plus, he's really big on an eye for an eye ... As for driving your ass to work and back, that's what Zee's for," he explains, reminding me of the card Zee gave me last night. He had told me to call him if I needed anything, and I considered it while my uncle was carving me up, but I didn't have my phone. "But it doesn't even matter 'cause you don't need to worry about money."

"Dude, quit being crazy. If I'm gonna move out, I need to make earning some money my top priority."

"No, you don't. You belong to us now and vice versa, so all of what's ours is yours, meaning our house."

What the shit? Is he being serious right now? He sure as hell looks like he is.

I promptly shake my head. "No effing way."

His lips spread into a grin. "Yes *fucking* way."

"No. There's no way in hell I'm moving in with you guys."

He juts out his bottom lip. "Why the hell not?"

"Well, for starters, I've known you guys for less than twenty-four hours. And I'm not a charity case. I can take care of myself. I have been for quite a while now."

"Oh, I know you can take care of yourself. You're one of the most strong-willed people I've ever met, which is saying a lot. But, as far as you not knowing us for very long, that doesn't mean anything. You can know people your entire life and still not really know them. While some people you've barely met, yet you feel like you've known them your entire life. It's how I felt when I met Zay and Jax. It was like the stars aligned and all that shit."

"How very romantic," I joke in an attempt to change the subject.

His grin broadens. "Isn't it?"

A soft laugh slips from my lips, a surprising noise after the heaviness we were just talking about.

"Your smiles are gorgeous," he tells me. "Do you know that?"

Uncomfortable with the compliment, I roll my eyes. "And did you know you have a weird obsession with my cheek?"

"That's because I'm an obsessive kind of guy. Once I decide I like something, I have to have it." He smooths his hand across my cheek. "But your skin's also really soft. I can't help wanting to touch it." He dazzles me with a flirty smile.

"You really know how to work that smile, don't you?"

He nods shamelessly. "And that's not the only thing I know how to work."

"Oh, good God," I groan, bobbing my head back. "Do you ever stop?"

He grins. "Don't pretend you don't think I'm amusing."

I want to tell him that he's not, but he really is.

When I make no effort to disagree with him, his grin

broadens, but then his smile fades as he brushes his fingertips along my side again. "I think you should tell Jax and Zay about this. But I'm not going to tell you that you have to—that's more their thing." He carries my gaze. "But if you do, I promise they'll understand. They get stuff like this. In fact, they have their own scars."

I squirm at just the idea of showing them. It was hard enough with just Hunter, who's the least intense of them all. "I'm sure they do, but it doesn't make it any easier. I mean, this—the scars ... the new cuts—it makes me seem weak and I'm not."

"I know you're not," he promises. "But I understand why you feel that way. I really do."

My gaze drifts to his side where I now know scars are hidden. "Why'd you show me your scars? You barely know me."

His lips tug upward. "Do I really need to give the barely-knowing-people speech again?"

I shake my head, smiling. "No, but ..." I waver. It's not that I don't believe him; it's just that, with some of the stuff I've overheard, I wonder how no one has seen his scars before. "Can I ask you something ...? It's about your scars."

He gives a hesitant nod. "Yeah, go ahead."

I scratch my wrist where another series of scars are

hidden. "How is it possible that no one else besides me, Zay, and Jax have seen your scars? I mean, from what I understand, you seem like the kind of guy who ..." Shit, how do I put this without seeming like a total perv? But the more I think about it, the more I realize being blunt might be the only option here. "Who likes to take his clothes off in front of others."

He wrestles back a smile. "You mean, I seem like the kind of guy who likes to fuck?"

I sigh. "Fine, yeah, you seem like the kind of guy who likes to fuck."

His eyes glint with amusement. "There are plenty of ways to fuck with your clothes on. It's actually really convenient for quick fucks, which is all I do. Plus, a lot of times when people fuck, the lights are off." He pauses, assessing me with a drop of humor in his eyes. "You're not going to blush on me, are you?"

"Nope. That's not my style."

"Such a shame." He sketches the pad of his thumb along my bottom lip then across my cheekbone. "I bet these cheeks would look even more gorgeous all flushed to match your innocence."

I quirk a brow at him. "How many times do I have to tell you I'm not innocent? I'm just as rough and badass as you guys. Yesterday on the bridge more than proved that. No, actually, I proved I was more badass since I jumped off while it was freezing, something none of you guys have done." I flash him a snarky smile.

He shakes his head. "You're so feisty. I think I really fucking like it." He stares at me, rolling his tongue in his mouth, a contemplative look on his face. "Can I ask you something?"

That curious look on his face has me wanting to say no, but since he was cooperative with my questions, I decide to nod.

"You said you've only *kind of* been kissed, right?" He observes my expression closely.

I nod, a little concerned with where he's going with this, if I'm going to end up having to explain how that doctor pressed his lips to mine once. Well, at least I think it was only once. My memories are a bit hazy when it comes to my time spent there.

"What did you mean by that?" he treads cautiously.

"There was this doctor at the psych ward I stayed at. He tried to kiss me once." I say it like it's no big deal, and as long as I don't think about it too much, it isn't. But when I think about it too much, it starts to consume me, and then the darkness inside me ends up seeping out, and I do shit like try to cut my wrists open to bleed the pain out.

His eyes widen. "What do you mean *tried?* Did he ...? Did he force himself on you?"

I start to shake my head then hesitate. "Honestly, I'm not sure. I mean, I can remember him pressing his lips against mine, but then he pulled back and that's about all I can remember ... I have other memories of him saying some weird stuff to me and looking at me for too long, but that's about it. But I have a shit memory, so ..." I shrug.

He remains quiet for a second. "Have you ever been diagnosed with anything for that?"

I shake my head. "Other than being crazy, nope."

A frown forms on his face. "I wonder if we should look into that."

"You mean, like have me go to shrink?" I swiftly shake my head. "No thanks."

He offers me a sympathetic look. "From what you just told me, I totally get your apprehension, but we can make sure to find a good one. One who understands that if he lays a hand on you, he'll lose that hand. And we can get one who specializes in memory loss."

"There are doctors who specialize in that kind of stuff?"

"Yeah. Zay actually had to go to one for a couple of months."

"Really? Why?"

"Because when he was about eight or so, he couldn't remember like two months of his life."

I think about the dream that I'm really starting to question if it wasn't a dream.

"Did they figure out what was wrong with him?" I ask quietly.

"No, but to be fair, he quit way before he was supposed to. Zay's never been really good with that sort of stuff, so no one was surprised."

I nod, understanding way more than I wish I did.

Silence skips by, the wind twirling around us and a bird caws in the distance, the noise causing goosebumps to sprout across my arms.

"So, how do you feel about it?" he finally asks, measuring my reaction closely.

"With seeing a therapist?" I ask, and he nods.

Well, on one hand, I hate the idea of being around a therapist again, but on the other hand, it might be nice to know what the hell is wrong with me, other than I'm crazy.

"Can I think about it?"

I tense when he wraps his fingers around mine. Then he trails his fingers down my hand.

"Of course you can." He sketches his thumb along the elevated scars that only Zay knows about. "Your uncle didn't do this to you, did he?"

How did he know they were there? Did Zay tell him?

I want to lie. Tell him he did put those scars on me,

too. But the lie won't leave my tongue, so instead, I shake my head. It's beyond annoying, this inability to lie to him. I think it might be that he's been so honest with me and it makes me feel guilty enough not to want to fully lie to him. Who would've thought some blond-haired charmer would be the one to crack the icy wall I built around myself?

Sadness masks his expression as he reaches up and molds his palm to my cheek. "I'm sorry you're in so much pain."

My heart is beating so loudly I can barely hear over it. I don't like this. Don't like him being able to see beneath my mask, able to see the ugliness all over me, inside me.

"I wasn't in pain. I was just … tired." Tired of my life. Of living in my own head. Of hating myself.

I don't like these feelings he's bringing out in me. I need to shut them down. Bleed them out if I have to.

He sketches his thumb along my skin. "That kind of tired can be painful."

"You say that like you're speaking from experience," I mutter, wishing we'd get off the subject of me.

"Maybe I am." He looks at me, and then he's leaning in and his lips are touching mine.

I tense. I should probably pull back. I know I should. Instead, I stand there, letting his lips linger on mine. It feels sort of good, not that I'd ever admit that. Still, it doesn't mean I should just let him kiss me.

I start to pull away, but then he slips his tongue inside my mouth and lets out a soft groan. Then leans back, his eyelids lifting open. He doesn't speak right away, but his expression is filled with a frenzy that matches the crazy thudding of my heart.

That was ... I don't even know ...

Scary?

Terrifying?

Hunter takes a breath and then another, slowly calming down, and I discreetly do the same.

"Don't tell Jax I did that." The corners of his lips kick up into a small but sad smile. "I mean, you can if you want to, but he's gonna be pissed we both just broke a rule."

"Hey, *you* kissed *me*. I just stood there." Thankfully, my tone comes out even or else he might figure out how much that kiss affected me. "And I don't know anything about these rules, nor have I agreed to obey them. But I won't tell Jax you broke his rules. But only 'cause I'm not really a rule follower."

His lips quirk upward as he muses over something. "You know, if I was Zay or Jax, I'd give you a big lecture about how you're going to obey the rules. But I'm not them, so I'm just gonna let it slide on by and say thanks for agreeing not to rat me out to big brother."

"Yeah, but if you were Zay, we probably wouldn't be in this situation," I retort, a grin pulling at my lips. "Since, from what I understand, he won't kiss anyone on the mouth."

This I can do. The joking and teasing. It's all the heavy stuff ... and the kissing ... that makes me feel like I've fallen off a cliff and will never land. Or I'm going to land soon and end up breaking into a thousand pieces. Who the fuck knows?

"True." He starts to smile, but it fizzles when Zay honks the horn at us. He sighs, seeming disappointed. "I guess that's our signal to head back to the car."

I nod and start to turn for the car, but he tugs at my hand.

"I'm not gonna force you to tell Zay and Jax about what happened to your side," he tells me again, "but I really wish you would. They'll be understanding with this. I promise."

He's promised me a lot of things over the last few minutes, and while I like his promises, I'm not sure if I believe them. Not with how many false promises have been thrown at me over the years.

Trust, it's a complicated thing that I'm not even going to try to pretend to understand.

I promise you'll be okay.

I promise you're gonna have a great life.

I promise things'll get better.

I promise you'll make it through this.

I promise I'm not going to hurt you. All you have to do is run.

Yeah, from what I know, promises are about as reliable as my memory.

7

RAVEN

Jax gets out of the car as we wander back to it. He doesn't ask any questions when he sees us, just glances between Hunter and me, his gaze dropping to our interlocked fingers.

Hunter gives my hand a squeeze then casually pulls away. Part of me is relieved he does it, while the other part of me longs for that skin-to-skin connection I've rarely felt in my life, not since my parents died.

Sometimes I can still feel the warmth of their blood on my hands and smell the scent of death in the air. It's weird that I can remember that part, yet I can't remember what actually happened.

"You good?" Jax asks Hunter as I'm ducking into the car.

"Aren't I always?" Hunter replies amusedly, but I think his amusement might be a bit forced.

It grows quiet after that as we all climb back into the car. I put my I-don't-give-a-shit-about-anything mask back on and my guard goes back up, but inside my stomach is twirling with regret as what happened in the trees catches up with me.

Why did I show Hunter my wounds and scars? Why did I expose myself like that?

"That took you two a long time," Zay mutters as he steers the car back onto the road.

"Worried you're gonna be tardy?" I joke as I sit back in the seat, pretending to be chiller than I am.

He narrows his eyes at me in the rearview mirror. "Do I seem like the kind of guy who'd care about that?"

"Well, you didn't seem like the kind of guy who'd jump into freezing cold water to save me, but you clearly are, so ..." I lift a shoulder.

His grip on the wheel constricts. "So you and me are gonna keep dancing like this? Good to know."

"Dancing?" I question. "Don't you mean me *handing you your ass?*"

His nostrils flare, and he starts to turn around in the seat to do who the hell knows what.

"Zay, focus on driving," Jax orders as he pushes a few buttons on his phone.

I find it a little bizarre that neither one of them have asked if I told Hunter what was wrong with my side. With Jax being so demanding about it, I thought he'd bring it up again. And Zay hasn't brought it up either, which again, is strange.

The only thing I can think of is that Hunter somehow told them without me knowing. But that doesn't seem possible since they haven't been alone together … unless he managed to send them a text without me knowing. If he did, that means he lied to me.

I sneak a glance at Jax, who's still looking at his phone, reading something on the screen. Suspicion builds inside me, and I'm about to go all interrogation on them when he sets his phone down.

"We need to talk about the rules," he announces, sticking his hand out toward Hunter. "Before I do, though, give me the box."

Hunter's eyes light up. "Shit. I almost forgot about that." Grinning at me, he opens the glovebox. "It's present time."

"Is it someone's birthday?" I ask, glancing at the three of them.

Hunter shakes his head as he collects a small box from inside the glovebox. "Nope. This is an apology present."

"No, it's not," Jax insists as he snatches the box from Hunter. "She just needs one. That's all."

"Aw now, come on, Jax. You can at least call it an apology present for breaking hers," Hunter tells him, closing the glovebox.

"Calling it that would mean I feel sorry for breaking it, and I don't." He hands me the box. "Besides, the one I threw out the window was a pile of shit."

Wait ...

I glance at the box he's holding out for me to take. A box that holds a fancy looking phone.

Confusion twirls in my mind. "You bought me a phone?"

"You don't have to sound so sad about it." Zay turns onto a wider road that's lined sparsely with houses. "In fact, you should be saying thank you."

"Why? You guys broke my old phone." I toss Jax an accusing look. "Or *you* did, anyway."

The corners of his lips quirk for a microsecond, but the look quickly evaporates. "Yeah, I did. But like I said, I'm not apologizing for it. You shouldn't have tried to call someone."

"Yeah, because it's so insane of me to want to try to call for help when three guys force me into an SUV," I quip with an eye roll. "I'll make sure to make a mental note of that for next time that happens."

"No," all three of them say, startling the crap out of me.

I suspiciously glance at them. "Why do you guys all look like you're planning on rehashing what happened yesterday?"

"We're not." Jax fiddles with a piercing in his brow, twisting the barbell a little. "But there's a risk that someone else might try to do that to you. It's how Honeyton works."

"Because of the whole five mafia families?" I ask, but it's not really a question. I figure that's probably the reason.

Jax nods then urges me to take the phone. "This, though, is going to help protect you."

I don't take the phone, still a bit suspicious. "Why? My old one didn't help protect me from you."

Again, his lips barely, *barely* quirk. "Only because it was a pile of shit. This one"—he drops the box onto my lap—"has a tracking app, something your old phone didn't have."

"I'm pretty sure that ancient piece of crap didn't even have the capability of getting apps," Zay remarks as he pulls into an old-school looking diner with flashing neon signs.

I'm not sure why Zay is parking in front of the diner, unless he's getting breakfast.

"It didn't," I clarify, still not picking up the box. I feel like the moment I do, I'm silently agreeing to some sort of commitment with their little circle. "But it's the only phone I could afford. And it made calls and texts, which is all I really need."

Hunter glances over his shoulder at me with his brows knit. "What about your social media accounts?"

I snort a laugh. "That's the funniest joke you've told yet, Blondie."

His lips part, and then he tilts his head to the side. "Did you just call me *Blondie*?"

Huh, I think I did. I guess I'm not opposed to nicknames.

"Yep. And I think it's pretty fitting." Grinning, I wink at him.

He narrows his eyes, but it's a playful move. "Why do I get the feeling you're secretly making fun of me?"

"How can it be a secret if I'm doing it right in front of you?" I bat my eyelashes innocently at him.

Instead of retorting, he smiles. "Aw, look. You did listen to what I said earlier."

I'm beyond confused. "Huh?"

His grin widens. "When I told you that if you batted your eyelashes at someone, you could get whatever you want."

I scrunch my nose, realizing he did say that to me. "That isn't why I batted them. And I wasn't even trying to get anything."

He muses over what I said, resting his arms on the back of the seat. "You're right, but still, I think you should get something out of it for looking so damn cute. So, what do you want? New shoes? A car? How about a unicorn? I think you mentioned something about that yesterday."

I make a big show of rolling my eyes. "Yeah, Blondie, I did, yet I still don't have one. Guess you're not as badass as you thought."

His smile is so bright I swear he's about to throw up rainbows all over me. "Give me a few days, and I'll make it happen." He flashes me one final grin before turning around, opening the door, and hopping out of the car.

Zay climbs out, too, as Jax flips up the seat but pauses before he gets out. "Take the phone out of the box and bring it in with you. We'll help you set it up while we're taking care of this other shit." Then he gets out without waiting for me to answer, as if expecting me to do what he says.

Part of me wants to leave the box on the seat, wants to keep my ass planted where I am, wants to put up a good protest; be badass, stubborn Raven. Because, while I've spent a lot of time being lonely, I've never wanted to be the sort of girl who just follows other people around. I was taught to be tougher than that. Like how my dad taught me how to throw a mean right hook, he also taught me how to be independent, to not rely on people, which has come in handy over the years.

But, as I get out of the car, I start to wonder if maybe I was just really good at being by myself because it was my only option. Or maybe I'm just curious about these guys. Or maybe the loneliness has finally broken me.

8

RAVEN

"Holy crap, it smells amazing in here," I say as I follow Zay and Hunter into the diner with Jax trailing along behind us.

The place is pretty empty, except for a waitress standing behind the counter and an old man drinking coffee in one of the leather corner booth. The air smells like coffee and waffles, and I breathe in the scent as I wander farther inside with my new phone in hand, waiting for it to power up.

I felt kind of stupid when I had to ask Hunter how to turn it on, but it's way fancier than I'm used to. Hunter smiled when I grudgingly asked for help and made a remark about me being cute before showing me which button to hold down.

I'm quickly realizing that, out of all of them, Hunter's

the one who's going to be the nicest to me. Although, he does have a mean streak. I briefly witnessed it when we were at the bridge. But I don't think he's nearly as intense as Zay, and definitely not as intense as Jax. And unlike Jax, Hunter is a rulebreaker. I can still feel him on my lips when he broke the rules only a handful of minutes ago.

Zay seems like a rulebreaker, too. And I definitely am, which makes me question what's the point of even having rules.

As I wander inside the diner, my phone screen lights up with a message about entering the login information for my account. Since I don't have one, I move to tap the new user button, but then Hunter lightly swats my hand away.

"Jax already set one up for you when he purchased the phone and linked it to our account." He drapes his arm around my shoulders. "We've got you, little raven."

I pull a wary face. "But, doesn't that mean you can, like, see all the calls and texts I make and monitor stuff on my phone?"

"Yep. Which is exactly how I want it." Jax steps up beside me, stuffing his phone into his back pocket. Then he looks at Hunter. "Help her set it up while you guys order. I gotta talk to Quinn for a few minutes."

Hunter snickers. "By talk, don't you mean fuck with her head and body?"

Jax shrugs, his gaze briefly zeroing in on Hunter's arm over my shoulders. "Make sure to keep your hands to yourself," he warns before heading past the scuffed-up tables and red leather booths and toward a hallway tucked in the far back corner near the labeled bathroom area.

I arch a brow at Hunter. "He's going to have sex with someone in the bathroom?"

Hunter removes his arm from my shoulders and takes my phone from me. "Kinda."

Question marks swirl through my mind. "How can you *kinda* have sex with someone?"

He pauses from typing in my login information and glances up at me then at Zay. "You wanna handle this one? Or should I? 'Cause, while I love talking about sex, I'm not a fan of explaining the fucked-up complication that is Jax's sex life."

Zay rolls his eyes. "Like yours isn't complicated?"

"I never said it wasn't. I just said that I don't want to explain Jax's to her." He shrugs. "Besides, I got account info to put in, waffles to order, and a unicorn to find. It's gonna be a long, hard day for Blondie." He flashes me a grin, and I shake my head but smile.

Zay grimaces, irritation masking his expression. "Fine, I'll try to explain it to her."

"Or you could just not," I suggest. "I don't really need

to know." But I'm kind of curious. Not that I'm going to admit that aloud, because yeah, that'd be fucking weird.

"Actually, you kind of do," Zay tells me while Hunter wanders toward the counter.

I shake my head as Hunter says something to a woman standing behind the counter. She isn't dressed in a waitress uniform, so I'm unsure who she is.

"Ever heard the term TMI?" I ask Zay.

"Yeah, but if you're going to be living with us, you're going to have a lot of questions when night rolls around." He draws the hood of his jacket off his head and scrubs his hand over his short brown hair.

"Why would I move in with you?" I ask. "That's crazy talk right there."

"Like Hunter didn't already make you the offer." Zay puts his hand at the small of my back and urges me to follow Hunter as he walks away from the counter and swings around the tables, heading toward a corner booth.

"How do you know he did?" I ask suspiciously.

"Because we discussed it last night," he says as he steers me past the empty tables. "And we know everything each other has done or did."

"That sounds weird and complicated."

"It is. Everything about us is, including you. And it's going to be really fucking complicated when you move in with us."

"Just because you guys discussed it, that doesn't mean I'm just going to move in with you. It's too ... weird." But weird might be an understatement.

"Weird or not, it's going to happen," he states matter-of-factly. "You'll want to eventually. And when you do, you should be prepared for the shit that goes on, 'cause we're not going to tone it down just because some girl's living with us."

My brow curves upward. "Worried I'm gonna ruin your bachelor pad?"

His eyes darken. "No, I'm worried you're going to freak out when you hear screaming in the middle of the night."

"I don't freak out that easily." I pause as what he said registers. "Wait. Screaming in the middle of the night? You guys got some sort of torture dungeon in that mansion of yours?"

"Kind of." He scans my expression then leans in, putting his lips beside my ear. "It's probably not the kind of dungeon you're thinking of. It's more of a playroom for Jax's complicated sex life."

"You know, I think you're trying to shock me right now, but it's not working," I tell him as I slide into the booth with Hunter, putting myself directly across from him.

Zay sinks down beside me and drapes an arm along

the back of the seat just behind me. The smell of cigarettes and cologne mix with the scent of breakfast lingering in the air. "I doubt that with how innocent your mind is."

I roll my eyes as I scoot over and put a bit of space between us. "I'm far from innocent, and I think you know that, considering you read all about me and my messed-up mind."

"Yeah, you're definitely messed up in the head," he agrees. "But, in some ways, you're really innocent. You'll have to get over that, though, if you're going to be part of our circle."

"Again, I never agreed to be part of your circle." I eyeball the menus on the table as my stomach grumbles, but since I didn't bring any money, I don't pick one up.

Apparently, Hunter finds my stomach grumbling amusing because he glances up from my phone with a big, old grin on his face. "Hungry? Or did you eat a baby gremlin this morning?"

"It was the latter," I lie, not wanting to let on that I'm starving. "And it was delicious."

He chuckles, shaking his head, then returns his attention back to my new phone. "So fucking adorable."

I give him a dirty look. "Stop saying that ..." I trail off as a younger woman with red hair, wearing a fancy black dress and heels, approaches the table. She has a smile on her face, but it's far from friendly. She also looks familiar, but I can't place from where.

"Boys," she greets the guys as she comes to a stop beside the table.

And just like that, the air around the guys changes, shifts, tenses, both Hunter and Zay going rigid as they glance up at her.

Hunter pales as he clutches my phone. "What the fuck are you doing here?" he asks in a startlingly clipped tone.

"I come bearing a message." Her eyes stray to me. "But I was also a little curious to see what all the fuss is about."

Zay slides his arm underneath the table and into his pocket. When he pulls his hand out, he's holding a pocketknife. "There's no fuss, so give us your message and get the hell out of here. This isn't your territory."

"Thank God for that," the woman replies with a repulsed face as she peers around the diner. "This place is a dump. It's part of the reason it was even given to you—because no one wanted it. Seems pretty symbolic if you ask me."

Wait ... Does that mean these guys own the diner?

What the actual shit?

Zay sets the knife on the table. "Tell us the message and get the hell out of here before we make you."

The woman rolls her eyes, but a drop of nervousness resides in her expression as she fleetingly glances at the knife. "Whatever. Like I even want to be here. I'm just doing my job."

"You mean, your job of playing my dad's whore?" Hunter smirks at her. He seems to have collected himself but still appears mildly pale.

Just who is this woman? His dad's mistress maybe? If it is, I feel sorry for him.

"Aw now, don't be jealous." The woman extends her perfectly manicured fingers toward him, and Hunter swallows hard.

"If you touch him, I'll slit your throat, Diane." Jax appears behind her with his arms crossed.

The woman—Diane—stiffens as she lowers her hand. Fear illuminates in her eyes, but she hastily collects herself before turning to face him and plastering on a sugary sweet smile. "Jax, so lovely of you to join us."

Jax stares her down hard. "Wipe that stupid smirk off your face, tell us the message, and get out before I make you."

She puts her hands on her hips. "Whatever. You're all just a bunch of spoiled brats."

"Isn't that like the pot calling the kettle black?" Hunter mumbles with a frown.

She glowers at him before she again collects herself,

smoothing her hands over her dress. Then her attention locks on Jax. "I was sent here to deliver a very important message, but it has to be in private, which is why he didn't send you a text."

"Go ahead and tell me," Jax demands. "You know whatever you tell me, I'll tell my circle."

"Yeah, but she"—she flicks a glance at me—"isn't part of your circle, is she?"

Jax's gaze sweeps across me then looks back at Diane. "Fine. Come with me." Then he starts across the diner again, heading toward the hallway that he went into earlier.

Once she's gone, Hunter lets out a shaky exhale.

"Who is she?" I ask, looking at him.

His frown deepens. "My stepmom."

"Oh." That wasn't what I was expecting him to say. "She looks young."

"She is young," Hunter mutters, slumping back in the seat. "My dad only likes younger women."

"Oh." I study him—how pale he looks, the uneasiness stirring through him. "You don't like her very much, do you?"

He shakes his head then picks up my phone from off the table. "I absolutely and utterly despise her more than I do anyone else in this world."

I can't help thinking of the scars on his side and

wondering if she was the one who put them there, but I don't dare ask.

"Who's she delivering a message from?" I ask instead, not really believing they'll tell me. But it doesn't hurt to try to get a bit more info from them. Maybe if I do, I can get to the bottom of why it seems like I know Zay.

"Our boss," Zay answers, stuffing his knife back into his pocket. "So basically, Jax's dad."

I nod like I understand, but I really don't. "Mobster stuff, I'm guessing?"

Zay gives me a curious yet amused look. "You say that so casually."

I rest my arms on top of the table. "I think I've already proven I don't get scared very easily."

"Yeah, you don't." He glances at my side. "You never did show Jax and me what happened to your side."

Not wanting to go back to that subject, I divert. "So, you guys own this diner?"

"Yep," Zay replies, cracking his knuckles restlessly. "But don't try to change the subject."

I tuck my arm to my side protectively. "Nah, I think I'm going to."

Zay leans in, parting his lips, but Hunter speaks first.

"If you want her to trust you, then you gotta give her a reason to," he tells Zay while pushing a few buttons on the phone. "Maybe if you show her your scars like I did, she'll trust you like she trusted me."

"Like hell I'm going to do that." Zay blasts him with an appalled look, then his eyes darken as his gaze lands back on me. "Besides, if I want to see her scars, I can. I don't need her permission."

"You do if you don't want your fingers broken," I throw back at him.

His lips curl as he slants even closer to me. "I'd like to see you try, princess."

"Then how about you try to lift up my shirt?" I challenge. "But let me emphasis on the *try* part, because you won't get very far."

He shakes his head in astonishment. "You still got that death wish, don't you?"

"Nah, I just really like breaking fingers," I quip. "Especially fingers that belong to a brooding douchebag who thinks he can always get his way."

Zay grips the back of the seat as he slants so close to me that our lips almost touch. I refuse to lean back, though. Refuse to lose whatever the hell this challenge thing is going on between us.

"Dude, I can't tell if Zay wants to hit you or fuck you, little raven," Hunter remarks with a pucker at his brow, his gaze dancing between the two of us. "Maybe a little bit of both."

Zay shifts his cold gaze to Hunter. "Don't," he warns.

"Don't what?" Hunter asks, batting his eyelashes innocently.

Zay curls his fingers into fists as he leans over the table. "Don't imply that shit."

Hunter taunts Zay with a smirk. "Imply what?"

Tension ripples in Zay's body as he shakes his head and slumps back in the seat. "You really get on my nerves sometimes. You know that?"

Hunter nods with a grin. "And yet, you still love me."

"That's debatable right now," Zay grumbles as he folds his arms across his chest, his attention drifting to the hallway where Diane and Jax went. "I really don't like that we're not back there with him," he changes the subject. "He should've taken us with him."

"You know he can't," Hunter tells him as he pushes a few more buttons on the phone. "Until our little raven takes the oath, she can't share in this part of our lives yet—not until she's vowed the Oath of Silence. But we couldn't just leave her out here alone either and Jax knew that. That's why he went back there with her. Besides, Jax can handle Diane."

So many questions flood my thoughts, one being: "Why can't I be out here by myself?" I flick a glance around the mostly empty diner. "There's literally, like, no one here. Well, unless you're afraid I'm going to rob your diner or something." I faintly smile. "Which honestly, doesn't sound like a bad idea."

Zay smirks at me. "Go ahead. It'll just give us a reason to chase you down and torture you."

I roll my eyes. "Yeah, yeah, you say that now, but when you actually start to go through with the torturing, my bet is you'll chicken out and save me."

Zay's eyes widen then narrow. "Keep it up and I'm gonna prove you wrong. In fact, I have duct tape and rope in the trunk that I can go get right now."

"Go ahead and try. I'll fight you," I tell him. "Just like I did yesterday."

"It didn't work out that well for you yesterday, though, did it?" he challenges.

I'm about to throw back a snarky comeback when Hunter interrupts.

"Zay, brother, friend of mine, you are getting in deep fast," he says with a grin, but a drop of nervousness resides in his eyes as he trades a look with Zay.

Zay grows quiet after that as he sinks back in the booth.

What is it with these guys and their coded conversations and looks?

Hunter gives Zay one more pressing look before fixing his attention on me, a smile gracing his lips. "We're not worried about you robbing us, though that'd be cute to watch." He stretches his legs out underneath the table, his foot bumping into mine, but he doesn't move it, leaving it resting there. "We're worried who might see you sitting here all by yourself."

"Again, I stress, there's no one here." I point at the old man sitting in a booth. "Well, except for that old dude, but I really doubt he'd try to do anything to me."

"Maybe, maybe not. And just because it doesn't seem like anyone else is here, that doesn't mean there's no one watching," Zay mumbles, pinching the brim of his nose.

My eyes widen. "What?"

Zay shrugs, lowering his hand to the table. "Someone's almost always watching you in this town. At least, that's the mentality you have to have because, more than likely, it's true."

"You mean, someone's always watching you guys?" I ask, glimpsing around the diner, wondering if there are cameras or something around. But that just seems crazy ...

Cameras are angled at me as I sit in the padded room with the doctor walking toward me ...

I yank myself from the memory, highly aware that my body is shaking.

"It's not just us," Zay says, and I do my best to focus on what he's saying, but the memory haunts my mind. "Everyone in this town is usually keeping an eye on each other. The people who are part of the five families do it to protect themselves, because anyone can attack at any time if someone pissed off the wrong person. As for the people who aren't part of the families, they still have to keep their guard up."

I recall something Katy said to me yesterday, about there being a lot of sexual assaults in this town that get dusted under the rug. "Why? I mean, what're they so afraid of?"

Zay leans closer to me, an almost menacing look dancing in his eyes. "Getting beat up, killed, raped, drugged, set up. If it's a crime, it's a risk here. And the police won't do anything about it. Either the bosses pay them off or get rid of them if they won't be bought off." He pauses, assessing me. "Does that frighten you?"

Hunter brushes his foot against mine, either playing footsies with me or trying to comfort me. "If you are, it's okay. We won't let anything happen to you."

"I'm not afraid." Although a tiny part of me is. But it's nothing I can't handle. "I'm just ... trying to figure out why this town works like that. I mean, how did five mafia families even end up here?"

"It's a long story," Hunter replies vaguely, "that involves a lot of corruptness, distrust, and backstabbing." He glances at something over my shoulder and his expression plummets. "And while you probably need to hear it, we don't have time right now."

I track his gaze and spot Jax and Diane exiting the hallway.

Diane instantly makes a beeline for the door, but she briefly catches my eye before she walks out. The smallest trace of a smile touches her lips then she pushes out the door.

Why the hell did she look at me like that? And why do I get the feeling her smiling at me is a very bad thing?

Jax takes his sweet time returning to the table. He has a knife in his hand, and when he reaches our table, he stabs it into the table then fixes his gaze on me. "It's time for you to take the oath. This can't go any further until you do. And if you're not going to, then you need to leave, because I have stuff to talk about with my brothers and I can't do that in front of you until you've taken the oath."

I glance from the knife stabbed into the table then up to him. Part of me knows I should be afraid with how much these guys seem to like pulling out knives, but I'm not. I don't know why. Don't know what's wrong with me.

"Dude, what the hell did that table ever do to you?" I ask, arching a brow at Jax.

Hunter snickers then sticks out his fist in my direction. "That one deserves a fist bump."

I bump his fist while Jax shakes his head and pulls his knife out of the table and sets it down. Then he fastens his gaze on me.

"No more jokes. It's time for you to decide," he tells me. "Either you take the oath and become one of us, or we take you home and you can forget everything that's happened. I'm not about to have secrets in this circle, but until you take the oath and make a promise of silence to us, I can't just say what I want and need to." He places his palms down on the table and leans toward me. When the scent of his cologne touches my nostrils, I have to admit that it smells really good. Almost as good as this diner smells. "So, what's it going to be? Are you going to run from us or fly with us, Ravenlee?"

It's weird to hear one of them say my real name.

I mull over what he's asking, conflicted. I've never been one for being put on the spot or for making decisions on the fly. Usually, I procrastinate for as long as possible. But I can tell that Jax means what he says.

The thing is, I'm still not even fully certain what I'm getting into if I take this oath and become part of their circle. All I really know about them is that they're part of the mafia, like to torture people, carry around knives, and they're impressed when people defy them and do crazy shit. Well, impressed enough to bring them into their circle.

"How do I even take the oath?" I ask. "I mean, what am I promising?"

Jax smiles. Actually fucking smiles. But it's not a

warm smile. No, it's completely and utterly sinister, a taunt that would make most freak the heck out. But I've seen a lot of scary stuff in my life, so I don't spook that easily. Then he slowly shakes his head. "No, if you do this, you go in blind. That's how it works."

I glance at Zay, who's watching me with a smirk, and then at Hunter, who looks amused and less pale than he did earlier. Then my eyes land back on Jax and his sinister smile. I really have no reason to trust these guys, and really, I don't. But a part of me, the one I pretend doesn't exist, doesn't want to be alone all the time anymore.

Freak.

Murderer.

Loser.

Maybe, just maybe, being part of their circle will put a stop to the whispers.

And besides, if I want to find out if I really know Zay without him knowing, getting close to him might be my best option.

"Fine," I say with a shrug, but it's mostly bravado. "I'll take the oath, but I'm not moving in with you guys."

As their grins grow, I worry what sort of fate I just sealed for myself, of what I'm about to lose. But not enough to back out.

And really, it's not like I have anything to lose.

9

RAVEN

After I agree, everyone sort of relaxes. It makes me even more concerned over what I'm getting myself into, but not enough to back out.

"So, now what do I do?" I ask after a couple of seconds go by and no one does or says anything.

"Now, you take the oath," Jax sinks down in the booth beside Hunter.

"And then we'll discuss this whole moving in thing some more," Hunter adds with a grin. "Because you can argue all you want, but it's gonna happen."

I feel like banging my head on the wall. *And I thought I was stubborn.*

"Yeah, but what does that entail?" I question suspiciously.

"What do you think it entails?" Hunter observes me with amusement.

I give a shrug. "I don't know. Letting you guys shove me off a bridge? Torturing me? Cutting me? The list of ideas filling my head is pretty endless."

"But they all share one trait." Hunter thrums his black-painted fingers against the table. "They're all morbid, which means you think we're morbid."

I shrug again, not bothering to even try to deny it. "From the first time I met you, you've threatened to hit me, push me off a bridge, make me your sex slave, and told me you were gonna kill me, tie me up, and torture me. So, why wouldn't I think that?"

"And yet, you're still here." Zay stretches his arm along the back of the booth, his fingers brushing my hair. "So, either you don't scare very easily or you like to be tortured."

"Wouldn't that be funny if she did?" Hunter muses, his gaze flitting to Jax.

Jax pins him with a threatening look, to which Hunter retorts with an impish grin.

Jax opens and flexes his hands, focusing back on me. "We're not going to do any of those things to you. In fact, I think we've stressed that we won't let anyone hurt you once you join our circle."

"Which includes you guys?" I ask dubiously, fiddling

with a saltshaker on the table, feeling really restless about the situation I just got myself into.

When Jax hesitates, Hunter chuckles under his breath and mutters something incoherently. Jax must hear him, though, because he gives Hunter a chilling look.

"Stop with the jokes," he warns harshly.

Hunter just rolls his eyes then shoves the sleeves of his shirt up, rests his arms on the table, and looks at me in all seriousness. "Jax is right. We're not going to hurt you. The oath is actually pretty simple. We're all just gonna tell you some rules and you agree to abide by them."

"There's also a task," Jax adds, causing Hunter to forcefully smash his lips together.

I eye them over apprehensively. "What kind of task?"

They've all grown a bit tense. Or, well, Hunter has. Zay isn't even looking at me, dazing off toward the counter. Jax just appears as indifferent as always.

Jax's lips part, but then the woman that Hunter spoke to earlier approaches our table with a round tray balanced in her hand and interrupts him.

She has grey hair that's pulled back in a braid and is wearing square-framed glasses, jeans, and a T-shirt. If she wasn't carrying food, I'd assume it was just someone here to talk to the guys, but because she is, I'm guessing she's the waitress. I just don't get why she's not wearing a uniform.

"Here ya go, bosses," she greets them as she sets the tray on the table beside ours. On the tray are several plates with various breakfast foods. She proceeds to put them on the table in front of us, humming along with the old school tune faintly playing from the jukebox.

"Thanks, Mable," Hunter tells her with a charming grin.

She grins back as she slides a plate containing a chocolate chip waffle in front of him. "You're welcome, honey. I put a little extra chocolate chips in there for ya, just the way you like it."

Hunter rubs his hands together as he grins at the plate. "You're seriously the best."

"You just say that 'cause I bring you food," Mable remarks as she places a plate of eggs and bacon in front of Jax. "And for you, Mr. Grumpy Pants, I put extra cheese in your eggs. Maybe that'll get you to smile. Probably not, though."

Jax glances up at her then does something completely wild.

He smiles. Like a real fucking smile.

"Thanks," he tells her as he picks up a fork.

I gape at the scene, literally having no idea what to do with the exchange.

Mable notices my reaction and laughs. "Jax smiling is a crazy sight to behold, isn't it?"

I give an exaggerated nod. "It's like seeing a unicorn or something."

Hunter smiles cleverly at me as he reaches for the syrup. "Look, I did make that happen for you."

I roll my eyes, ignoring the grumbling of my stomach. "Unless Jax has a horn hidden somewhere on his body, he's not an actual unicorn."

A wicked grin spreads across Hunter's face. "Well, he doesn't *technically* have a horn, but he has a c—"

"That's enough." Jax's smile is no longer visible as he picks up his fork. "That'll be all, Mable."

Mable rolls her eyes as she sets down a plate of pancakes in front of Zay, who shockingly also smiles at her. Then he dives in, stuffing his mouth with food.

"Don't try to dismiss me, Mr. Grumpy Pants," Mable scolds Jax, wagging her finger at him. "You can try to act scary, but I've known you since you were a baby, and I can still remember the time you shit your pants because you were too damn scared to walk into the bathroom by yourself."

I press my lips together as a laugh bubbles up my throat, but a snort still escapes me.

Jax's cold gaze slices into me, his lips parting, but Mable places a hand over his mouth, silencing him in a similar way he's done to me multiple times.

"Don't you dare disrespect her," she warns Jax then

looks at me. "Since these boys have no manners, I guess I'll just introduce myself. I'm Mable. I used to be their nanny. Now I run their diner. Although, I sometimes still have to keep an eye on them since they clearly haven't learned any manners yet, even though I've tried to teach them many times."

I can't help smiling. "I'm Ravenlee."

"Ravenlee," she muses with a smile. "That's a really pretty name."

"Thanks." I fiddle with the leather band on my wrist as she momentarily assesses me.

"So, how did you end up with these hooligans?" she asks curiously as she places some glasses of orange juice in front of everyone.

I glimpse around at Hunter, Jax, and Zay, who are all looking at me warily. I wonder what they'd do if I told her the truth. Part of me is curious to find out, to see if she scolds them. But I decide to let them off the hook.

I flash the guys a grin as I recline back. "I'm new to Honeyton," I tell her. "And they're being kind enough to show me the ropes of this lovely little town."

She chuckles as she picks up the last plate on her tray. "I like your attempt to bullshit me, Ravenlee, but I've known these boys long enough to know the word *kind* is never applied to them." She sets the plate down in front of me.

I glance down at the waffle, eggs, and sausage, my mouth instantly salivating. But, as hungry as I am, I can't pay for this food.

"Um, I didn't order anything," I tell her, moving to hand her back the plate.

"I ordered it for you." Hunter reaches across the table and swats my hand away from the plate before I can pick it up. "If you don't like what's on it, we can order you something different. But I think you should at least try the waffle." He grins at Mable. "Mable makes the best waffles."

"I make the best everything," she quips, scooping up the tray. "I need to go fill in another order. If you guys need anything else, get off your asses and get it yourselves." She walks off toward the counter.

"She's funny," I remark with a small smile.

"She is. And kind of crazy." Hunter picks up a fork. "Which is why we like her so much. Even Jax has a soft spot for her."

Jax shakes his head as he shovels a bite of eggs into his mouth, but he doesn't argue. Instead, he looks at me. "We need to get you to take the oath so we can finish our breakfast and get to school." He scoops up another forkful of eggs. "We're going to tell you the rules, and afterward, you need to agree to them. Then we'll give you the task to complete. After that, you'll officially be part of our circle."

"And what if I don't want to agree with one of the rules or this task?" I ask. "Then what?"

Jax stuffs the forkful of eggs into his mouth. "Then you can get up, walk out of here, and forget your time with us. Although, I stress, if you run your mouth about anything you've heard us talk about, we'll have to punish you."

"You don't need to worry about me talkin'," I tell him. "I'm not Dixie May. And besides, I'm not much for making friends."

He studies me for an unnerving beat. "We'll see. But, just know what happens if you don't accept the oath, because I don't fuck around." He leans forward, resting his elbows on the table. "I will punish you if you talk about us with anyone, which just happens to be the first rule of the oath: what happens in the circle, stays in the circle."

"That one doesn't seem so bad," I inform him, trying to ignore the mouthwatering scent of the waffle.

"So, you're agreeing to it?" Jax double-checks as he picks up a slice of bacon.

I nod. "Sure."

"Good." He bites off a chunk of bacon. "Hunter, you're up."

Hunter looks at me. "I'm gonna tell you the next rule, but while I do, eat up."

"I'm not hungry," I lie, my stomach churning in protest.

"Liar." He pushes the plate closer to me. "Your stomach's been grumbling all morning."

I resist a sigh. "Look, I appreciate it, but I'm not gonna eat food I can't pay for."

Hunter's mouth tugs up into a half-grin. "You don't have to pay for it."

I push the plate toward him. "I already told you that I'm not a charity case."

"This isn't charity." Hunter shoves the plate back at me. "We own the diner, so we eat for free."

I tuck my hands to the side, refusing to touch the food. "Yeah, but I don't own the diner."

"Oh, for the love of God, I can't take any more stubbornness," Zay says then reaches over with his fork and cuts into the waffle.

I expect him to take a bite, which is why he catches me off guard when he moves the fork toward my lips and stuffs it into my mouth. A protest works its way up my throat, but then the taste of the waffle touches my taste buds and ...

"Holy shit! This is so, so good." I moan.

Smirking, Zay sets the fork down on my plate. "Maybe you should start listening to us more."

"She definitely should." Hunter dives into his own

waffle. "Which brings us to rule number two: you're to always listen to what the other circle members have to say, even if you don't want to hear it."

"It doesn't mean I always have to do what you tell me to do, though, right?" I reach for the bottle of syrup. "Because I can't agree to that."

Strands of Hunter's blond hair fall into his eyes as he shakes his head. "Nah. But sometimes you might have to back us up, even if you don't want to."

I consider what he's saying. Can I do that? I think so ... "Okay."

Hunter gives me a pleased grin. "Good. Now take another bite of your waffle."

"Is this your attempt at being bossy?" I quip with an arch of my brow.

He grins back at me. "Yeah. How'd I do?"

I stuff another bite of waffle into my mouth. "Good enough to get me to eat. Although, that might be because these waffles are so freakin' yummy."

He grins then shoves a mouthful of waffle into his mouth before glancing at Zay. "You're up, brother."

I twist in the seat to face Zay who's looking at me with his arms crossed, his jaw working as he chews.

"Rule number three," he states. "You will always have our backs, even when you don't agree with us. But you'll always support us, even when shit hits the fan, which it will."

Again, that doesn't seem so bad. "All right."

A flicker of surprise sparks in his eyes, probably because I'm being agreeable. But the look fades as he goes back to eating.

"And rule number four and the last rule," Jax says, drawing my attention to him. "You'll never stab us in the back. *Ever.*"

"Okay." Again, these rules don't sound that bad. "Is that it?"

Jax nods but then wavers. "Well, and the one I set yesterday about everyone remaining friends."

"Okay," I repeat, kind of surprised about how easy the rules are.

Honestly, with how big of a deal they were making it out to be, I thought they were going to be way more intense.

Jax nibbles on his lip ring, his gaze dissecting me. "Now, for the task."

"Aw, yes, the task," I remark, stabbing my fork into a sausage. "If this task is anything like the rules, I should be fine with it. Although, I have to say, you guys really over-hyped the rules. Seriously, it's a bit anticlimactic."

Jax's lips slightly twitch, either with annoyance or amusement—I can't tell. My guess is the latter.

"The task is simple in theory. Though, I'm a bit doubtful you'll be able to pull it off," he taunts, probably trying to get a rise out of me. And it works.

"I can pull off anything if I want to." I flash him a cocky grin.

He barely smiles. "I guess we'll find out."

"I guess we will," I reply haughtily. Then I realize he hasn't even told me what they want me to do. "Wait. What am I supposed to do?"

Jax's smirk is all cruelness. "We need you to seduce someone for us."

I blink at him. "Come again?"

His smirk turns even crueler. "There's a guy named Porter Aversonly. He's the nephew of one of the bosses of another mafia family. A while ago, our bosses gave us the task of befriending him in order to get some information about his family. However, Porter is a complicated guy."

"Which basically means he's a douchebag," Hunter says as brushes strands of his hair out of his eyes. "I've been trying to make friends with him for a while. I even joined the basketball team that he's on, but Porter's too cautious a guy. He's an asshole for sure, but he also knows to keep his guard up around members of other families."

"You're on the basketball team?" I question, giving him a once-over.

"What?" he asks with hilarity. "Don't I look like a jock?"

I snort a laugh. "Fuck no. And if you did, I wouldn't be sitting here."

"Why? You got something against jocks?" he questions with his brow cocked, a smile playing at the corners of his lips.

I shrug, nibbling on my sausage. "I know it's kinda stereotyping, but from past experiences, jocks are jerks. Plain and simple."

"So you try to avoid them," Hunter scrubs his hand across his jawline musingly. "And yet, you're sitting here with three of the most dangerous guys in town, one of which may or may not be a psychopath." He gives a not so subtle nod in Jax's direction.

Jax doesn't remark on Hunter's comment. He simply focuses on me. "So, do you accept the task? Or are you too afraid?" he taunts. Again, I think he's trying to get a rise out of me.

I chew on my bottom lip. "I'm not afraid, but I really doubt I'm going to be able to seduce a jock and get him to spill all his secrets. And what info am I even supposed to be getting from him? I mean, what do your bosses want to know?"

"They want to know why the Aversonly family has been so fucking quiet," Zay explains then takes a sip of his orange juice. He winces when he puts the glass back down onto the table and his arm bumps against the corner of the napkin dispenser. I wonder why. "It's not like any of the families to ever be quiet, so it's an anomaly."

"It's a warning is what it is," Hunter mumbles as he pours more syrup onto his waffle. "They're up to something. Something that's probably going to fuck the rest of the families in the ass."

"This family stuff is sorta confusing," I interrupt as I grab a napkin from the dispenser. "And wouldn't my lack of knowledge be a problem when trying to seduce a guy who's part of this whole mafia families' thing?"

Hunter shakes his head as he sets the bottle of syrup down on the table. "Porter won't give a shit about that. All he's gonna care about is that you're gorgeous and easy."

"But I'm not—"

"We need to explain more about the families to her," Jax talks over me. "We need to take a day to do that ... Maybe tomorrow."

"But there's school tomorrow," I point out, wiping some syrup off my fingers. "And while I'm okay with ditching occasionally, it'll only be my third day here. And I missed half the day yesterday, thanks to you guys being crazy. And now I'm already tardy this morning."

"Both of those things will be excused." Hunter winks

at me then crosses his fingers. "Remember, me and Mrs. M are like this."

"Who's Mrs. M?" I ask in confusion.

"The secretary you were talking to when the fates finally decided to like me." Hunter's smile is as bright as the neon signs hanging around the diner.

I'm still not following him. "Why'd the fates start liking you then?"

He wets his lips with his tongue then nibbles on his bottom, hesitating. "Because it was the day I met you."

Zay releases a loud exhale. "Don't start with this fate shit again."

"No way," Hunter starts, but Jax talks over him.

"Both of you don't start," he warns then looks at me with his hands overlapped in front of him. "Now, do you accept the terms of the oath or not?"

I scratch my scars. "It's not that the task scares me or anything. I just really don't see myself being able to seduce anyone, let alone some douchebag jock. And I'm not gonna sleep with him. I may be a daredevil with some stuff but prostituting myself is where I draw the line."

"Actually, it wouldn't be prostitution since we're not paying you," Hunter points out, and I roll my eyes at him. But he only grins. "And we don't want you to sleep with him. We just want you to fuck with his head a bit and make him think you're going to."

"I think you're overestimating my ability to charm someone over," I stress. "That's more Dixie May's thing. I usually rub people the wrong way. You guys should know that already since I managed to piss you all off the first day I met you."

"Actually, you just pissed Zay off," Hunter reminds me. "And honestly, I think he was more shocked at your defiance than pissed off."

"I wouldn't go that far," Zay mutters as he wipes his fingers off on a napkin. "But I do think she might be able to pull it off with a little bit of training."

"Dude, I'm not a dog," I tell him as I pop a chunk of sausage into my mouth.

"I'm not saying you are," Zay replies, tugging at the sleeves of his shirt. "But you're gonna have to learn to be more cooperative if you want this to work."

"Why would I want this to work, though?" I question. "I mean, all that's really in it for me is that I get to become part of you guys' circle. Which, according to you, offers me protection. But honestly, the only threat I've seen so far is you guys."

"Which mean, if you're not in our circle, we're a threat to you," Jax stresses as he finishes up the last of his eggs. "Something you should consider before making your decision."

"Is that a threat?" I ask, carrying his gaze.

He shrugs. "You already know enough about us to know that we're a threat to anyone outside of our circle."

True. And that should be enough for me to walk away. In fact, I should just get up now and do that. Forget I ever spent any time with these guys. But I can't bring myself to do so.

I try to convince myself that the reason I can't is because I want to find out if I've ever met Zay, if there's any truth to the dream I had last night. In reality, that's only part of the reason. The other part has a lot to do with the curiosity of what it would feel like to not be totally alone anymore. Not that I think me and these guys are going to become BFFs, despite what Hunter says. But it might be nice to have someone else in my life, besides an aunt, uncle, and cousin who hate me. And these guys seem okay with the whole murder thing, which should be a warning flag, but honestly, so am I.

Murderer.

Freak.

Monster.

Alone.

Alone.

Alone.

I skim my finger along the inside of my wrist, along the elevated scars. "Even if I agree to try to complete the task, I still don't think I'm the right kind of girl to seduce a jock."

"I can teach you a few things about seducing," Hunter offers as he shoves his empty plate into the middle of the table. "I've been told I can be quite charming sometimes." He winks at me.

"I'm sure you have." I roll my eyes but then sigh. "But I think that kind of charm is a gift and can't be taught."

He dismisses me with a flick of his wrist. "You have it in you. You just need the opportunity to explore it a bit."

I lift a brow. "And you're gonna help me with that?"

He nods. "Absolutely."

They momentarily fall into silence after that. I'm not sure what they're waiting for. For me to agree to this task? For me to run out of the diner?

"So, do you accept the oath?" Jax finally asks, watching me closely.

Every part of my mind screams at me to say *no*. That I won't be able to pull it off. That I don't need to. That I've handled being by myself for years and can keep handling it.

But then I skim my fingers along my scars again, remembering the agony, the emptiness of each passing day, of not wanting to get up, of having nothing. And I'm tired of having nothing. I'm tired of being in pain. I'm tired of being tired.

Maybe I'm crazy for doing what I'm about to do. I have spent the last several years being told I'm crazy. So, I tell myself I'm just living up to my reputation.

"All right," I say. "I accept the oath."

They all grin. Even Jax cracks the smallest of smiles.

I'm not sure if that's a good thing, but I guess I'm about to find out.

"But I'm not moving in with you," I add, just to make sure we're on the same page.

No one says anything, but by the looks they give me, I know I'm gonna have a fight on my hands. Not that it matters. Yeah, I may have taken the oath, but I'm not going to rely on these guys for everything nor will I let them take care of me. Sure, it'll be okay to not have to be totally alone while I'm living in Honeyton, but in the end, I can't trust someone that much. Plus, I'm always going to take care of myself.

"Don't rely on anyone," my mom told me only hours before she died. "You're a strong girl. Always stay that way, okay? You can't trust people. They're evil. Evil is every-where, Raven. Even in places you'd never expect."

My parents said that to me a lot, and I always nodded, not fully understanding what they meant. But now ...

I understand them more than I wish I did.

10

RAVEN

"You really don't have any social media accounts?" Zay asks me as we wait for some apps to download onto my new phone and for Hunter and Jax to get done doing what Hunter referred to as "boring office shit."

"Nope. I've never had a reason to have them." I glance up at him. "I can't believe you have them, though. You don't seem like the type to air your personal shit out into public."

"I don't post a lot of shit," he explains as he stacks our dirty plates. "But I do have some accounts—everyone does."

"Except for me," I remind him as I set the phone down on the table.

Man, downloading apps takes forever.

"Nope. Not except for you." He taps his finger against

the screen of my phone then starts stacking the empty cups. "You, princess, have officially become a member of online social media."

"Awesome," I say flatly. "Honestly, I'd rather not be. It's not like I have anything to say. Plus, I don't want people knowing my personal shit."

"Then don't post anything."

"Okay, then what's the point of creating the accounts?"

He shrugs, rotating sideways so his knees are touching mine. "It's a way for us all to communicate with each other if we needed another form besides text. Plus, we can keep track of each other that way. And, we gotta play the part."

"The part of what?"

"The part of us that we show the world," he says, tossing dirty napkins onto the stack of plates.

"As opposed to the part of you guys that the world doesn't see?" I collect the rest of the dirty napkins.

He lifts a shoulder as he takes the napkins from me. "I think you've already caught on that we all have two sides to us. The one we show the circle and the one we show the world. And I know you have two sides to you, too, so don't pretend like you don't."

"I'm not pretending. I'll admit I have a ton of sides to me, but no one ever sees most of them."

His gaze fleetingly zeroes in on my side. "Is that where you keep one of your sides hidden?"

I tuck my arm against my side. "Maybe."

His gaze lifts to mine. "I think Jax should've made you show us what you've gotten hidden underneath your shirt ... He should've made it part of the oath."

I flash him my pearly whites. "But he didn't, so I don't have to."

He eyes me over warily. "You know, you've sassed off to me more than anyone else ever has. It's making things really complicated." He tugs on a strand of my hair then quickly pulls back like he didn't mean to do it. "Maybe if you were more cooperative, things would be easier for you."

I dismiss him with a flick of my wrist. "Nothing about life is easy. At least, not with mine, so why would I ever think that?"

He shakes his head. "Just show me what's on your side."

Great, he's still on that. "Why?"

"Because it's driving me crazy."

"Again, why? Why does this matter so much to you?"

"Because ..." He yanks his fingers through his hair, the strands going askew. "If you'd just tell us, then maybe we could take care of whoever hurt you."

"You're already supposedly gonna take care of my

uncle. And Hunter says he's gonna take care of Dixie May. So just how many people are you guys planning on taking care of for me?"

"As many as we need to."

I assess him. "You always act like you like *taking care* of people. Is it really that fun for you?"

His lips tug upward into a smirk. "It is, so why don't you tell me who hurt you so I can get a little pleasure today as I tear them apart?"

I feel like I should be afraid of his words, but I feel nothing.

Absolutely nothing.

"Maybe no one hurt me ... Maybe I did this to myself." It might not be true with this new wound, but I have hurt myself before.

He tenses then hurriedly rises to his feet, tugging at the sleeves of his shirt. "I'm gonna go give Mable the dirty dishes. Stay right here," he says then picks up the plates and cups and rushes toward the counter like he's completely afraid of me. But I really doubt that's true. I doubt Zay's afraid of much of anything.

Leaning back in the booth, my thoughts drift to my own fears. Fears I'll never admit aloud because, like I already told Zay, I have a ton of sides to me. And the side that feels fear I keep hidden away as much as I can;

hidden way deep inside me, almost beside all my forgotten memories—

Ping.

An incoming text comes through, my very first message, but who the heck could it be from? It's not like I've given out my phone number to anyone. Well, I guess Hunter, Jax, and Zay probably have it, but wouldn't they just come talk to me?

Confused, I open the message, and my stomach plummets.

Unknown: Hello Ravenlee, welcome home. I should warn you, though, that Honeyton isn't your typical place. Everyone has secrets, just like you. And I'd advise you not to trust anyone with those secrets. In fact, I'd advise you not to trust anyone at all if you want to play the game right. And be especially careful around The Raven Three.

"What the heck is this ...? Who sent this ...? And what game ...?" I trail off as an audio file pings through. The title: *Welcome Home.*

Every one of my instincts begs me not to press play, but curiosity gets the best of me. I tap my finger against the screen.

A haunting song starts to play from the speaker, and I suddenly feel like I'm flying away ...

My hands are around someone's throat. I'm squeezing hard. So hard I can almost feel bones breaking. A scream pierces the air. I want to stop, but I can't. I have to listen to it—

I blink back to reality as the song stops playing. My pulse is racing, and I feel as though I'm about to crawl out of my skin.

"What the hell was that?" I whisper, my finger hovering over the play button as I contemplate playing the song again. However, I move my finger away as Hunter approaches the table.

His nostrils look a bit red, and he's sniffing like he's got a cold, but he wasn't like this earlier, which makes me wonder if he was snorting lines.

"Is everything okay?" he asks as he plops down into the booth beside me and drapes his arm around my shoulders.

I debate whether or not I should tell him about the message. Part of me wants to, but it did warn me about being careful around the guys. I have no idea who sent it, though, so how can I just trust some random message?

I'm really thinking about showing him, but when then I glance down at my phone again, the message isn't there.

What the hell?

I glance up at Hunter and find worry is written all over his face.

"What's going on in that pretty head of yours?" he asks, tucking a strand of my hair behind my ear.

I think about telling him, but the words *trust no one* flash through my mind, and I find myself shrugging. For now, I'll keep it a secret, but I'll look into the warning more.

What the hell was that song anyway?

"It's nothing," I lie, putting my phone on the table. "I'm just thinking about—or, well, dreading—going to school."

He smiles. "Don't worry, little raven; we've got your back. Nothing bad is gonna happen to you." He pauses, rubbing his lips together. "Hey, can I see that pendant you found in the field?"

"Why?" I ask, a bit confused at the swift subject change.

"I'm just ... It kind of reminds me of a pendant my sister had when she was younger."

Oh. "You have a sister?" I ask, retrieving the pendant from my pocket.

He nods, taking the pendant from me. "Yeah, she's just over a year older than me." He examines the pendant with a pucker between his brows. "You'll probably get to meet her soon. She stops by the house sometimes." He smooths his thumb over the pendant then hands it back to me. "It's not hers."

"It'd be kinda weird if it was," I tell him, stuffing the pendant back into my pocket. "Or, at least, it'd be weird if it was hers and my uncle was trying to burn it in the middle of the night."

"Maybe he wasn't trying to burn it," he says. "Maybe it just happened to be out there in the field by where the fire was."

"Huh? I hadn't thought of that." I doubt that's the case.

No, this pendant means something to me.

"I'll be right back," Hunter tells me with a small smile as he starts to get up. "Jax just send me a text and says he needs my help with something."

I know he's lying because he never took out his phone. But he doesn't give me time to point that out, hurrying away from the table.

I sit there in silence, trying to figure out what's going on when the entrance door flies open and a raven flies into the diner.

"What the hell!" Mable shouts as she rushes out from the kitchen.

The raven does a quick circle around the space then dives toward me. I duck, covering my head with my hands and closing my eyes.

Flap...

Flap...

Flap...

Feathers everywhere ...

Don't worry. We're in this together ...

My hands around their throat...

Blood on my hands...

Hurt them.

I start to get to my feet.

Flap...

Flap...

Flap...

I blink from the memories as the air grows quiet again. I glance around and the bird is gone, and Mable is closing the door.

"Jesus," she mutters as she turns to me. "Are you okay, honey?"

"Yeah, I'm fine," I lie in a shaky tone.

What the hell was that? Why did I feel like... Well, almost like I felt on the day my parents died, as if I dazed off and forgot about everything.

She gives me a quick glance over, like she doesn't believe me. "Well, I don't believe in curses, but if I did, I'd say my diner just got cursed."

"Or I did," I mutter quietly enough that she doesn't hear me. "It flew after me."

And unlike Mable, I believe in curses. So what does a raven flying over my head mean? That I'm cursed again? That I'm going to kill again?

Blood on my hands...

Hurt them...

Kill them...

I swallow hard as for a brief instant I swear I can almost feel myself squeezing the life out of someone. And all that fills my mind in that moment is the noise of flapping wings.

11

HUNTER

I'm TRYING TO BE AS CALM AS POSSIBLE, AND LUCKY for me, I'm a pro at that sort of shit. But eventually, the restlessness becomes too much, so I leave Raven to go back to the office where Jax is. As I enter the hallway, though, he's just exiting the office.

"Let me guess," he says when he sees me. "Everyone's restless to get to school and you came here to tell me to hurry up?"

I shake my head, my chest feeling extremely tight. "No, that's not even close."

The uneasiness in my tone makes him instantly tense. "What the fuck is wrong now?"

I glance nervously over my shoulder then shove him back inside the office, shutting the door behind us. "You ..." I pause, trying to choose the right words that won't make both of us lose our shit. Because the subject I'm about to approach is a touchy one for both of us.

Jax crosses his arms, trying to appear calm but tension is flowing off him. "Just spit it out."

Releasing a loud breath, I slump back against the door. "You remember that time in our life when our fathers made us ... play that game... And there was that girl they would bring in ... And we ... And we ... Well ... I mean, I can't remember much of it, but I know we ..." I can't even say it aloud. It's why I rarely let myself think about it. Because the guilt crushes me. I blow out a shaky breath. "But anyway, remember how we gave her that necklace? And then not too long after that, she stopped being brought to the house and we never found out why? Well, Raven picked up a feather pendant from off the ground this morning when she wandered out into the field. At first, I thought there's no way it could be the same one we gave that girl. But then I looked at it just barely and ... it has that indent in it that Zay accidentally made with his knife when he was trying to carve our initials into it but then gave up because it was too complicated to put them on such a small object."

Silence stretches between us, and my stomach starts to churn.

What if I'm right?

What if it is the pendant?

Memories start to trickle through my mind.

People are watching us, and a fire burns in the background, a song playing from the stereo ...

"What if this has to do with the game?" I say quietly after Jax says nothing.

He doesn't seem as shocked as I expect him to me. "Raven's uncle is from here," he says, surprising the hell out of me.

I gape at him. "When did you figure this out?"

He shrugs. "Like five minutes ago after one of my connections sent me a file about him."

My chest feels really tight. "If he's from here, then Raven's dad could be too, which means..."

"I know."

"Which means she has a connection to this town."

"I know."

"Which means she could've been here the last time our fathers had that stupid game going."

"I know all of this already," Jax says, briefly growing quiet. "There was something else in that file too... Apparently, Raven's uncle was part of this group that ran experiments here in Honeyton and one of those experiments had to do with hypnosis. It didn't list who else was part of the experiment, but I can't help thinking it might be our fathers, which would mean..." He trails off, not finishing.

I feel like invisible fingers have wrapped around my throat. "When did this take place?"

"I'm not sure... a lot of information on the documents were blacked out... but if we were somehow part of this experiment and so was Raven then I really doubt it's a coincidence we all ended up together again. I just don't know why or how. I mean, I know we ended up with her because Zay was pissed at her, but I thought it was kind of weird how he acted so obsessed with her straight from the beginning."

"Me too," I agree. "But if we know Raven from our past, now it sort of makes sense."

"Yeah... maybe..." Jax mulls something over. "But what's the point of all of this? Why bring us all back together after so many years have gone by? And why would my dad have me look into Raven and her uncle and his family if he already knows them? And wouldn't they expect us to find out about this experiment thing?" He sighs. "Unless I'm wrong about all of this."

"But what if you're not?" I mutter. When he frowns, I add, "Do you think... Do you think our little bird knows?"

He shakes his head. "I doubt it... If she did know, she wouldn't be here with us. Not after what we did." He presses his lips together, trying to keep himself under control. "And besides, I'm still not one-hundred percent positive she is the girl."

I hope he's right, but doubt weighs in my mind. Like Jax said, coincidences in Honeyton don't exist. The families control everything, have for a very long time, which more than likely means they're at least aware of the experiment that went on.

"I'll look into this more, but let's keep this between us for now," Jax says, reaching for his flask, his hands noticeably shaky. "I don't even want Zay knowing about it until I know what's going on."

I nod in agreement. Yeah, we're supposed to tell each other everything, but this might not be something Zay can handle. In fact, I know it isn't, or else his mind wouldn't have made him forget.

Honestly, we've all tried to forget those days when our fathers made us play what they called "the game," although what happened was far from a game. There are still triggers that occasionally appear that tug at what little memories I have, like the sound of a certain song, the flapping of a bird's wings, feathers ...

That's when I can see the people who were there, watching what we did, but their faces are blurry and misshapen. Sometimes, I swear I can even feel them still watching me ... can hear that song that was always playing ... that haunting tune that would make me zone out. When I'd come to, I'd have the awful feeling I did something terrible.

While I've never flat-out said it, sometimes I wonder if I was hypnotized during the game, which makes what Jax told me even more creeper. And it would explain why I can't remember much about what happened. I have heard rumors that our bosses were into that sort of stuff, like they've brainwashed the people who worked for them and their enemies. But I've never heard anything about an experiment.

"Hunter, if Raven is the girl," Jax says, drawing me from my thoughts, "then we ..." He presses his lips together, silencing himself.

But I know what he's going to say.

If it turns out Raven is the girl, then we probably don't need to worry about us breaking her anymore, because we might've broken her a long time ago.

That much about the game—or maybe experiment—I can remember.

12

RAVEN

After the bird flies out of the diner, I decide to go to the bathroom. Not because I need to piss, but because I need to pull myself together.

"Where's the restroom?" I ask Mable as I get to my feet.

"It's back there, honey." She points back at the hallway Jax and Hunter went down.

I have no clue where the hell Zay is. Still in the kitchen, maybe? But I can't see him back there.

"Thanks." I head in the direction she pointed in, winding around tables. When I reach the bathroom door, I turn the doorknob, but pause as I hear music floating from somewhere.

What the hell? Are Jax and Hunter back there having a party or something? Do they even care about getting to school this morning? The moment I mentally ask myself that question, I realize the answer is, probably not. And I usually don't care about that sort of stuff, but like I said earlier, it's my second day at this new school and I already missed half the day yesterday and part of this morning.

I should just go in there and tell them to take me to school. Get some space from them and clear my head. After that message I received and with how weird everyone's acting, I should want some space from these guys.

Yeah, I'm gonna do that, I tell myself as I turn away from the bathroom and follow the sound of the music to a cracked open door at the far end of the hallway.

I knock first, even though the door isn't completely shut. My knocking causes the door to open enough that I can see inside the room.

Hunter is in there, sitting on a table, cutting lines. Wisps of his blonde hair hang in his eyes as he focuses intently on the task, which is probably part of the reason he notices me right away. The music is also up really loud, so I doubt he heard the door open.

So I was right about why his nose was red.

Not that I'm one to judge. Still, I have to question if that's why he seems like he's always bursting with energy. It makes me wonder what he's like when he's not all jacked up on coke.

I'm thinking about him way too much.

Shoving thoughts of him aside, I mull over what to do next, if I should go in and tell Hunter I need to get to school or should I go find Jax or Zay instead?

I'm still deciding when Hunter leans down and snorts a line. As he straightens, his eyes are shut and for a moment, he looks blissfully content. I know he's getting high, but for a drop of an instant, I feel a bit envious of the look.

I should've smoked more this morning. I feel too clear headed right now.

Internally sighing, I start to back out of the room when Hunter's eyelids lift open. His gaze locks on mine and for a flash of a second, he appears guilty, which is kind of weird. But that look swiftly erases and curiosity sparkles in his eyes.

"What're you doing back here?" he calls out over the music.

"I need to get to school," I reply loudly, inching my way into the room, my gaze bouncing back and forth between the lines on the table and him. "But I have a feeling you don't plan on going to school today."

His head tips to the side. "Why not?"

I point at the lines. "Because class has already started and you're back here doing that."

A slight smile pulls at his lips as he hops off the table. "Getting high isn't going to stop me from going to school, little raven. I'm surprised you'd think that because I'm pretty sure you were high when we picked you up this morning."

"I don't think getting high is going to keep you from going to school," I explain. "I just mean that you're sitting back here chilling and snorting lines when we're way late for school. And no one else seems that eager to go, so I'm starting to question if you guys plan on going at all today. And it's cool if you wanna ditch, but like I said earlier, I have to go."

"And I already said I can get you out of getting into trouble for missing school."

"So you're not going to go then?"

He shrugs. "Maybe. Maybe not. It all depends on how long Jax ends up taking."

My brows knit. "What's he doing? Screwing this Quinn person? Which FYI, why haven't I seen this Quinn? Does Jax have her like locked in the office or something?"

"Nah, he was never actually fucking Quinn. We were just messing with you. Quinn's just a person who works here. She's probably in the kitchen right now." Hunter steps closer to me, amusement twinkling in his eyes. "But why did you say that like Jax might actually have some person locked up?"

"Because the way you guys talk about him it seems

like it could be a pretty realistic possibility. Plus, considering what you guys did to me yesterday... Anything seems possible when it comes to you guys."

"And yet you're still here," he says amusedly.

I shrug. "Yeah, but I'm also not that smart either."

"I doubt that. In fact, it seems like there's a lot going on in that pretty head of yours." He pauses, chewing on his bottom lip. "Maybe you should share some of it with me."

I lift a brow. "You want me to share what's going on inside my head? For reals?"

"Yeah, for reals." He grins. "What's so weird about that?"

I eye him over suspiciously, thinking about the text I received earlier, warning me to be careful around The Raven Three. "I don't know... I just... Why? Why would you want to know what's going on inside my head? Zay's looked up enough about me that you guys know about my background, so you know it's creepy as fuck... that I'm creepy as fuck."

The corners of his lips quirk. "We're creepy as fuck."

"Yeah, true." Still, I'm a bit suspicious of why he's trying to get me to open up to him.

He reduces the space between us until the tips of his boots touch mine. "Guess that means we're all gonna be creepy fucks together. So tell me creepy little fuck," he winks at me and I shake my head, fighting back a smile. "What's going on in that creepy as fuck mind of yours." He reaches out and grazes his knuckles across my cheekbone.

For some dumbass reason, my eyelashes flutter. It annoys the hell out of me. I mean, I just got a text from someone warning me about these guys. Although, it could've been some rando who sent it. Who the hell knows. I honestly feel like I don't know anything anymore. Like my life has been cracking apart beneath me for years and it's about to shatter. And I have no damn clue where I'm going to fall.

A smirk starts to form on Hunter's face, so I step back and swing around him, trying to pretend like I didn't just get all flustered from him touching me.

"Lots and lots of creepy things," I assure him, wandering toward the table. "I'm not gonna tell you any more about me, though. I'm all shared out for the day." I come to a stop in front of the table and stare down at the thin, white lines, remembering how blissfully content Hunter looked right after he snorted some. I want that feeling. Usually, I can smoke enough to get it. But I didn't do enough this morning, and now I'm stuck dealing with everything, and part of me just wants to go home where I can lock myself in my room and pretend this day never happened. That I'm just a normal girl that doesn't have a mind crammed with images of murder, who has normal friends, who doesn't have trust issues, who doesn't zone out for no reason.

I want to be normal. But how the fuck can I know what normal is if I've never had it? My life wasn't even really normal before my parents died. Even before I had that weird memory/dream with Zay in it, I thought my life was sort of strange. While other kids spent their time running around, playing games and hanging out, I spent time with my dad learning how to fight. I knew how to kick the shit out of someone by the time I was seven. And by the time I was eight, my parents had a game plan for a quick exit if someone broke into the house, like they were expecting something bad to happen. It's like they were always preparing for something, but I don't know what that was, other than maybe they were afraid of me and their exit plan was to protect them from me.

See this is why I don't share the creepy shit that goes on in my head.

"No way." Hunter moves up behind me, drawing me away from my thoughts. "Sharing time is only getting started. In fact, I'm ready to spend the entire day talking. Fuck going to school. Let's have some fun today."

"Easy for you to say." I cast a glance at him from over my shoulder. "You're all jacked up on coke." I twist around to face him. "So unless you want to let me do a line, I think I should go to school."

He eyes me over. "You do coke?"

"No. But so what? I get high all the time."

"Yeah... That's a little different, though. I mean, that's legal in a lot of places anymore."

I roll my eyes. "Are you seriously about to give me a lecture on doing drugs? For reals?"

"No," he replies with a roll of his eyes. "But I don't think I want to be the one to get you into this shit."

"You're not getting me into anything," I stress. "I'm asking to do it."

He studies me closer. "Yeah, but why? I mean, why did you just decide you wanna do it?"

I lift a shoulder. "Why does there have to be a reason? Maybe I just want to. Maybe I haven't done it because I haven't got the chance to do it before." I could just tell him the truth, that I didn't smoke enough this morning, and I have way too clear of a head right now. But then I'd have to explain why I like my mind foggy and that would lead to me telling him about all the stuff that goes on in my mind.

He cocks a brow. "Is that true?"

"I don't know." I give an indifferent shrug. "Maybe if you let me do it, I'll be chatty enough to tell you."

His gaze dissects me. "You know what, little raven? I have a feeling you're playing me right now, but it's impressive enough that I'll play along." With a bit of hesitancy, he steps back and shuts the door. "And I'm starting to think that I might not have to teach you very much to get you to be able to seduce Porter. I think you might have the game down already, whether you realize it or not."

There's that word again. *Game.*

He returns to the table, picks up a driver's license, cuts a thin line, and turns to me. "You sure you wanna do this? Because we can just go to school. In fact, maybe we should just go..." He trails off as I lean down and sniff the line up my nose, doing it the way I've seen people do in movies, which kind of makes me pathetic, but it works, so...

"Well, okay, then. I guess you just made the decision," he mumbles as I stand back up straight.

"I'm always going to make decisions when it comes to myself," I tell him, sniffing a few times. "When I can anyway." My nostril is burning and so is the back of my throat. "Dude, all this shit did was make my sinuses and throat ache."

"Give it a second," Hunter watches me with a wary expression on his face.

"Why're you looking at me like that?" I ask, rubbing my nose. "Like you're doubtful it's going to work on me or something?"

"That's not how I'm looking at you." He gives a short pause. "I'm just thinking I probably shouldn't have let you do that... I'm not sure why I did other than you're really hard to say no to."

"Dude, we already went over this—you didn't *let* me do anything. I *chose* to do it. And you've said no to me like ten times already, so that statement's completely inaccurate. Although, I haven't really listened to you when you said no, so maybe it's not." I start walking around the room, noticing all the framed artwork on the walls; photos of landscapes, people, and objects. It's just like at their house. "Did you take these photos too? They're really good. They kind of look like the ones at your house..." I trail off as he moves up beside me with a slightly amused smile on his face. "What did I say?"

He shakes his head, continuing to smile. "Is your nose still burning? Or are you feeling better?"

I note that my nose does feel okay now. "It's not burning as much. Is it supposed to? I'm still not sure if that was normal or not, since you never said anything."

He chuckles softly. "You're saying plenty for the both of us, sweetheart."

Great. Is he going to start calling me sweetheart now?

But that thought quickly becomes distracted by the realization that I've been yammering for about a minute straight. "Oh." I touch the heel of my hand to my forehead. "My brain's moving really fast."

Hunter smashes his lips together. "That's supposed to happen, honey."

And now he's calling me honey?

Le sigh.

I shake my head. "I know." I blink a few times, my eyes feeling super dry.

With a contemplative look, Hunter drapes his arm around my shoulder. "Want to go sit down and talk?"

I shake my head. "Nah, I'm too restless to sit."

"Then what do you wanna do?"

"I don't know... run a marathon."

He bites back a smile. "That might sound fun right now, but trust me, if you do it, you'll regret it when you come down."

"Well, that doesn't sound like fun," I pout with my lip jutted out.

He shakes his head with his teeth sunk into his bottom lip. "God fucking dammit, you gotta stop doing that."

"Doing what?"

He reaches up and drags his thumb along my bottom lip. "Pouting. It's gonna make me break the rules."

"Again, you mean?" I say with a smirk.

"Fuck," he groans. "You're gonna get me into a lot of trouble, aren't you?"

"Maybe. But I have a feeling it's gonna be a mutual thing."

"Perhaps."

We share a smile, and it's so easy, but kind of sucks because deep down, I know when the high wears off, everything is going to be heavy again.

"So if we can't run a marathon," I say, trying to distract myself from my thoughts, "What're we going to do?"

"Talk about the creepy as fuck stuff going on in your mind, remember?" he reminds me with a grin.

I dismiss him with a shake of my head. "Nah. I don't want to talk about that."

Now he's the one to pout. "Why not?"

"I don't know... It's just too weird, even with my mind racing like this."

He considers something momentarily then guides me over to a sofa near the far back wall and pulls me down with him as he takes a seat. "How about this," he says with his arm still draped around my shoulder. "You share one thing about you that no one knows and then we can do one thing that you want to do."

"Even if it's run a marathon?"

"Yeah, but I really hope you change your mind about that."

"I might, but maybe not." I consider what he's asking, and part of me wants to say no, wants to question why he wants me to share stuff about myself. But my mind's racing so fast that I can barely grasp onto the worry. "What do you want to know?"

He tilts his head from side to side, considering. "I don't know... How about what your life was like as a kid, before you moved in with your uncle."

I frown. "You want to know what my life was like before I killed my parents?"

He frowns too. "From what you and Zay have told me, I'm pretty sure you didn't kill them."

"Well, I'm pretty sure I did."

"No, I think you've been told so much that you have that you've started to believe it. But from the info Zay dug up, I don't think you did. Plus, you're free so other people must've thought that."

"There just wasn't enough proof," I mutter, wishing he hadn't brought this up.

It's ruining my high.

"Which could mean you're innocent."

"Or guilty, but there's just not enough proof."

He sighs. "Fine, I'll let this go for now, but you still

haven't answered my question. And if you don't then I can't do what you want." He gives an innocent shrug.

I roll my eyes. "Fine. Whatever." I sink back in the chair. "Honestly, my life wasn't too bad before... everything happened. My mom was really kickass. She could hold her own in a fight... I looked up to her." I miss her too, but I keep that to myself, despite how much my mind wants to pour out my heart and soul right now.

"What about your dad?" he asks, combing his fingers through my hair.

"He was cool too. He taught me how to throw a punch and what cars were considered cool, at least in his eyes. He was actually kind of a conman. I'm not really sure about everything he did—I was too young to remember—but I overheard my mom and him talking once about how if he ever got caught doing what he did, he'd go to jail."

"But you don't know what for?" he asks cautiously.

I shake my head. "Nah, but honestly they may have said why. I just might've forgotten." I tap my finger against the side of my temple. "Remember how I told you this thing is unreliable?"

He studies me with his brows furrowed. "Did you... Has your dad... or you ever been to Honeyton before?"

Warning flags start popping up everywhere.

Why would he ask that? Did Zay recognize me and tell him?

I could ask. My mind is hazy enough that I may have, but the words won't leave my lips. Literally. It's like the connection from my brain to my mouth shorts out and refuses to reboot unless I stop thinking I'm going to talk about that.

What the shit?

So all I can do is give a shrug and say, "I have no idea."

He bobs his head up and down absentmindedly. "Okay."

"Why did you ask?" I wonder, measuring his reaction carefully.

He gives a half-shrug. "No reason." He wipes the distracted look off his face and focuses on me. "You seemed like maybe you were happy back then... Back when you lived with your parents."

"I was." As guilt crushes my chest, I clear my throat. "All right, I've shared enough about me. It's time for you to pay up."

He hesitates then a mischievous smile touches his lips. "Okay, little raven, what do you want to do with me?"

I tap my finger against my lips. "Well, my first thought is to go to a bridge and make you jump off it." I grin.

He grins back, slanting closer to me. "If that's what you want to do, then I'm in. But just know that I'm not that great of a swimmer either, so unless you want me to drown, you might want to bring Zay with us so he can save me."

"Maybe I don't care if you get saved."

"Maybe you don't, but I'm betting you do." He waits for me to argue, and when I don't, his grin broadens. "I knew you liked me."

"Like is a strong word," I tell him. "I just don't hate you enough to want to see you drown."

"Is that so?"

I shrug. "Sure. Why not?"

He smiles and so do I.

But my smile quickly turns to curiosity, "Can you really not swim?"

"Yeah, pretty much. Well, I mean, I can kind of doggy paddle, but that's about it."

"Are you afraid of water?"

"Not necessarily afraid, but I'm not a fan of it."

"Yeah, me either."

"Yeah, I could tell that yesterday."

"Hmmm... I wonder why?" My tone oozes with sarcasm.

"Me too." He plays dumb and I roll my eyes, causing him to grin. "But for reals, what do you want to do, because eventually Jax is going to come look for us and then fun time is over."

"Who says I'm going to pick something fun for us to do?" I tease.

His all sorts of wicked amusement as he leans in. "Everything with me is fun, sweetheart."

"And cheesy apparently."

He presses his hand to his chest. "Hey, I prefer the term amusingly funny."

"I'm sure you do, but I like to go with the blunt truth." I pat his arm and offer him a sugary sweet smile, but then sigh. "Honestly, I don't really know what to do. I'm kind of lame when it comes to having fun."

He tangles his fingers through my hair again. "I doubt that."

"Doubt all you want, but it's true," I say. "But you seem like the kind of guy who has a lot of fun... Maybe too much. So tell me fun guy, what do you think we should do? I mean, what do you usually do when you're high and you need to burn off all this racing energy?"

"First of all, there's no such thing as too much fun." He points a finger at me and grins. "And second of all, you don't want to do what I usually do when I'm high."

With a clear head, I may have been smart enough not to ask, but all I want to do right now is find out, so I say, "No, I want to know."

He stares at me for a beat, his expression unreadable. "Fine, but don't say I didn't warn you." He shifts his weight, scooting closer to me and leaning in so his lips are beside my ear. "Usually, I fuck."

"Oh." I should've known.

He leans back, his gaze skimming across my face. "Fuck, I was hoping you'd blush."

"Well, I didn't and I'm not going to." Even if I kind of feel a bit restless inside.

He frowns disappointedly. "Such a shame. One day, though, I'm going to make it happen."

I roll my eyes. "Doubtful."

He smiles deviously. "We'll see." He leans back a bit. "So unless you want to let me pop your cherry, I suggest you come up with something for us to do."

I give him a *seriously* look. "Pop my cherry? Really?"

"I was hoping saying it'd make you blush," he admits.

"Well, it didn't." I chew on my bottom lip, thinking about what to do, my mind so clear from my worries that it's crazy. Honestly, at the moment, I feel like I could do just about anything.

Hunter's gaze zeroes in on my mouth. "You've got to stop doing that."

"Doing what?"

"Biting your lip..." He brushes the pad of his thumb along my bottom lip. "Pouting out your lip... Anything with your lips..."

The touch sends tingles through me, the sensation

startling even with the drugs buzzing through my body. I feel bolder, though, right now, like I don't have a damn care in the world.

"Why? Are you gonna kiss me again if I don't stop?" I ask with a quirk of my brow.

Okay, I must feel super relaxed if that sentence just left my mouth and I don't even feel weird about it.

He bites his lip so hard I swear he's gonna draw blood. "Don't tempt me... I already broke that rule once today."

"Like you care—" My words are cut off as he dips his head and brushes his lips across mine.

My breath gets caught in my chest as the move totally surprises me. But I was just taunting him so I don't know why I'm surprised. What I want to know is why I was taunting him. Why do I feel a connection to him?

"God, you feel so good," he mumbles with his eyes shut, his lips a sliver of space away from mine. "But I should stop, right?" He sounds severely conflicted.

I should nod. It's not like I trust him. Not really, anyway. But I don't trust anyone, and my mind's too free of doubt to really give a shit about much right now.

So I brush my lips against his.

Yeah, me, Ravenlee fucking Wilowwynter, just kissed a guy.

What the hell is happening to me? This town and these guys are breaking my head.

But that thought quickly gets sidetracked as Hunter lets out a soft groan, cups my cheek, and presses his lips to mine again. This time his tongue slips inside my mouth and I gasp like a spazz. But he either doesn't notice or doesn't care, kissing me deeper as he starts to guide me back until I'm lying down on the sofa. Then he lines his body over mine, groaning as his tongue slips into my mouth again. Even high, I feel way out of my element as I clutch onto his sides, holding onto him, my muscles wound up in knots.

"Relax," he whispers against my lips, pulling back slightly to look me in the eyes. His pupils look dilated, and I wonder how out of it he is—and how out of it I am. "You're doing fine. You just need to relax."

I bob my head up and down and loosen my grip on his sides, about to pull away and release him from my death grip.

"Keep touching me, though," he whispers, shutting his eyes.

His statement seems a bit odd since my hands are right by his scars, and he told me he never lets anyone see them. But maybe he doesn't mind people touching them? I don't know. And I don't really have time to over analyze it as he kisses me again, a deep groan reverberating through his body.

I put my hands back on his sides, his shirt riding up

just enough that my palms graze his flesh. Skin-to-skin contact, there it is again. And it's still as wonderfully terrifying as the first time it happened. Hunter must think so too because he shivers then deepens the kiss, his hand finding the bottom of my shirt and sliding up my side, his skin searing hot. Luckily, it's the side that's not scared or else pain and memories might have managed to burn through the drugs. But I wonder if it's the drugs that's making me okay with him touching me like this. Would I do it completely coherent? Who the hell knows since I've never made out with anyone before.

"I can stop if you want," he whispers against my lips. When I don't say anything, he leans back and searches my eyes. "You seem like you're not enjoying it... I should stop... right?"

"No... It's not that... I just don't know what I'm doing," I admit then want to kick my own ass.

Jesus, Raven, you sound like an idiot.

"You're doing fine," he assures me, stroking his fingers along my flesh. "Just try to relax more." His fingers skim up and down my side again as he leans in. "Relax," he whispers right before his lips touch mine.

I try to do what he says and chill the hell out. The more he strokes my side, the easier that is to do, which is weird. I barely know him and from what I do know, I should be freaking the hell out. Yet, I start to calm down enough to try to kiss him back. When my tongue touches his, he lets out a soft moan, his fingers splaying across my stomach. Then his hips grind against mine. Another groan from him, so I grind my hips against his. He lets out a shaky breath. I don't know why, but I like the noise.

"Good God, you're going to fucking kill me, aren't you?" he murmurs.

A snarky comeback tickles at my tongue, but he smothers it with another kiss, his tongue tangling with mine in an out of control kiss, his hands wandering up and down my sides, his hips moving with against mine.

Holy shit. My mind can barely process what's happening. Maybe if I could, I'd stop it. Maybe I'd remind myself why I'm cautious around people. Maybe I'd remind myself that I don't deserve to enjoy stuff.

I almost pull back as doubts creep through the haze in my mind, but then someone clears their throat and Hunter's pulling away.

"Fuuuck," he mutters under his breath.

He meets my gaze for a split second, and I spot the hint of worry in his eyes. Then he's pushing off me and sitting up. I follow, smoothing my hands over my hair and tracking Hunter's gaze to the door, which is now open. And Jax and Zay are standing in the doorway.

As usual, Jax looks completely indifferent with his

arms crossed as he leans against the doorframe. Zay, on the other hand, is shaking his head

"One fucking hour," Zay growls to Hunter with his fingers curled into fists. "That's how long it took you to break the rules."

"Actually, we set that rule last night," Hunter points out, folding his arms across his chest. "We just reiterated it to Raven an hour ago."

"Fine, then it took her one fucking hour." Zay's dark gaze shifts to me, so intense, so full of anger.

"If it makes you feel any better, that's not a record for me." My mouth moves on it's own accord—apparently I'm still riding my high. "When I was in third grade, my teacher gave us a list of rules on how to take care of our class pet bird. One of the rules was we weren't supposed to open the cage door because it would fly away. And like one minute later, I opened the door, and it flew out the window. But in my defense, I was trying to free it... I thought it seemed sad in the cage. But I was really into animals being free back then... Still kind of am..." I press my lips together, realizing I'm rambling and that they've all gone quiet.

I feel like an idiot until Hunter smiles at me, his lips parting. But before he can say anything, Jax speaks first.

"In the office. Now," he tells Hunter and Zay then turns and walks out, like he just expects them to obey.

And Hunter does, getting up to leave. Right before he walks out, he glances over his shoulder at me and offers me a small smile. But I detect a drop nervousness in his eyes.

Zay gives me another dirty look then he follows after Hunter. And he shuts the door behind him, leaving me sitting alone in the room.

The moment the quietness sets in, the last hour or so catches up with me as my high fades and I return to reality. Snorting lines... letting Hunter kiss and touch me like that... It's all racing through my brain, along with a distant memory...

The man brushes his lips against my cheek and strokes my head. "My little bird... You belong to me."

The memory snaps like a broken rubber band, but leaves my skin crawling. I want to cut out the sensation, let it bleed out until I feel nothing.

I can't do this.

Can't keep remembering this shit.

I need to block it out.

Spotting a razor blade on the table, I jump to my feet, grab the blade, and roll up my sleeve.

Then I make small cuts in my skin, but this time I can't keep the memories from surfacing, of the doctor, of the bird, of blood...

"What's happening to me?" I whisper as fear clenches in my chest.

I don't know why I feel this way or why I'm suddenly remembering forgotten memories, but one thing's pretty certain.

Coming to this town has sparked something inside me. And I need to find out why.

13

HUNTER

I'm so riled up I feel like I'm about to burst from my skin, which more than likely means this little meeting with Jax and Zay is going to get intense.

As we all enter the office, I prepare myself for an argument and to have to put up a lame ass attempt at defending myself for kissing Raven.

And touching her...

Jesus, I'm so turned on I can barely stand it.

Of course, Jax being Jax decides to drag out the anticipation as he shuts the door and sinks into silence.

"So how are we gonna punish him?" Zay asks as he sits down on top of the desk and crosses his arms. He looks like he's raging. My bet is he's pissed off that I kissed Raven. Not because I broke the rules, but over something else he won't admit. But he'll play it off as the rules thing

I roll my eyes. "I don't know why I need to be punished at all. It's not a big deal."

"You broke the rules," Zay snaps, his eyes narrowing to slits. "Which means a punishment is in order."

I roll my tongue in my mouth, getting more annoyed by the second, even though I know he's right. "It was an accident," I say with a lame shrug.

"What? You accidentally fell and your lips landed on her's?" Zay grumbles, opening and flexing his hands, on the verge of snapping. "Come on, even you have to know how fucking stupid that sounds."

"I never said that's what happened," I argue, stepping toward him. "I just said that it was an accident." Which is kind of true. I mean, I was high and so was Raven and she's so damn alluring... I felt like I couldn't help myself...

I never can, though, which is why I sleep around so much.

Fuck. Reality starts to set in. That I just kissed and touched Raven, and normally, this would be the point where I bail.

What the hell did I just do?

I need to fix this. Somehow.

"I can't believe this," Zay mutters, shaking his head. "Or well, I guess I can. You wouldn't be you if you didn't screw up like this."

"Like you haven't screwed up," I point out. "And why do you even care so much, man."

"Because you broke the rules," Zay bites out, the vein in his forehead bulging.

I roll my eyes. "Yeah, I'm sure that's the only reason."

"That's enough," Jax orders in a firm tone.

Grimacing, I turn to him and wait for whatever punishment he's about to give me. I'm sure it's going to be a bad one too, and maybe it would've been if the town's notification system didn't sound off at that very moment, which is never a good thing.

The system was created due to the high corruption in this town as a way of letting citizens know if an incident has happened.

As all of our phones go off simultaneously, we dig them out of our pockets.

Town Notification Alert System: Due to this morning's incident, the town has been put on lockdown. Please check the town's website for more information.

None of us check the website, though, since the information will be sugarcoated.

"Let me see what's going on," Jax mutters as he dials a number.

Zay and I nod, then trade a worried look.

"Maybe we should—" Zay starts, but he's cut off by a soft knock on the door.

With his brows furrowed, Zay walks over and opens it.

Raven is standing on the other side.

"Hey," she starts, fidgeting with the leather bands on her wrists. "I just got this weird alert message from the town and I'm not sure why."

"It's because something bad has happened," Zay replies in a cold tone.

I'm about to go over and interrupt their conversation so Raven doesn't have to put up with his asshole attitude, but then his voice softens a bit.

"It's probably not a big deal," he adds. "Some groups probably just got into a fight and they're just sending everyone home to clean up the mess."

Raven's brows rise. "Okay... um... Well that's weird, but whatever... Does one of you want to take me home then?"

"You're moving in with us, remember?" Zay reminds her in a haughty tone I've only ever heard him use with her.

Raven rolls her eyes. "I never agreed to that... And besides, I'm sure after the rules were... um... broken..." Her gaze briefly flicks to me and I can't stop a smile from turning up on my lips.

But the smile quickly fades as Jax reaches over and smacks me upside the head.

"Ow." I give him a nasty look. "What the hell was that for?"

"Do I really need to answer that?" he questions with an arch of his brow.

My lip twitches in annoyance, but I shake my head.

"Okay then." He turns to address everyone. "So apparently some sort of outbreak has happened and we're being told to go home and stay inside until further notice."

Raven's eyes widen. "What kind of outbreak?"

Jax shrugs. "Well, more than likely the police are going to say it's a virus or something, but really, a batch of tainted drugs probably got dealt and is giving people really bad side effects. And they've put out a notice for everyone to stay indoors so they can clean up the mess privately."

"I don't..." Raven trails off, shaking her head. "This town is so fucking weird."

"That it is. And this is barely the tip of the weirdness," I say, causing her gaze to stray to me again.

As our eyes lock, she bites down on her lip and my body pulsates.

Shit. I'm so screwed.

"We need to get to the house before the police show

up and force us to lock ourselves in here," Jax says while stuffing his phone into his pocket.

"Yeah," Zay and I both agree.

Because the last thing we want to do is be cooped up in this restaurant for who the hell knows how long—these lockdowns can sometimes go on for days.

"Can you guys drop me off on the way?" Raven asks, leaning against the doorframe. "Or are you gonna make me walk?"

"You're coming to the house with us," Jax tells her. As her lips part in a protest, he steps toward her. "That isn't up for argument. We probably have like maybe twenty minutes before the cops start making rounds to make sure everyone is inside, and it'll take us that long to drive to our house, so we don't have time for detours."

She frowns. "But then I'll be like stuck in your guys' house for a while."

"Yeah, so?" I chime in. "Our house is awesome."

She continues to frown with hesitancy written all over her face. "Are you sure you guys want me there?"

"We wouldn't have invited you if we didn't." Jax ushers her toward the door. "Come on. We need to send everyone home and lock this place up before we leave."

"Fine," Raven grimaces, but deep down, I swear I see a bit of relief in her eyes, like she's glad she doesn't have to go home.

And I'm completely on the same page with her. I think anyway.

Honestly, I'm kind of worried about what's going to happen with all of us being crammed under one roof. I just hope the lockdown doesn't last very long. But I guess it'll give us time to get to know more about Raven. I'm just worried what we'll end up finding.

ABOUT THE AUTHOR

Jessica Sorensen is a *New York Times* and *USA Today* bestselling author who lives in the snowy mountains of Wyoming. When she's not writing, she spends her time reading and hanging out with her family.

ALSO BY JESSICA SORENSEN

The Falling Series:

A Pact Between the Forgotten

The Ravens & the Mysterious Town

Untitled (coming soon)

Guardian Academy Series:

Entranced

Entangled

Enchanted

The Forest of Shadow & Bone (the start of Dash's story)

Entice

Untitled (coming soon)

Chasing Hadley Harlyton:

Chasing Hadley

Falling for Hadley

Holding onto Hadley

Untitled (coming soon)

Enchanted Chaos Series:

Enchanted Chaos

Shimmering Chaos

Iridescent Chaos

Untitled (coming soon)

The Breathing Undead Series

Breathing Lies

Shadowed Whisperers (coming 2019)

Capturing Magic:

Chasing Wishes

Chasing Magic

Untitled (coming soon)

Unexpected Series:

The Unexpected Complications of Revenge

Untitled (coming soon)

The Heartbreaker Society:

The Opposite of Ordinary

My Cursed Superhero Life:

Grim

Untitled (coming soon)

Tangled Realms:

Forever Violet

Forever Stardust

Untitled (coming soon)

Curse of the Vampire Queen:

Tempting Raven

Enchanting Raven

Alluring Raven

Untitled (coming soon)

Unraveling You Series:

Unraveling You

Raveling You

Awakening You

Inspiring You

Fated by Darkness

Untitled (coming soon)

Shadow Cove Series:

What Lies in the Darkness

What Lies in the Dark

Untitled (coming soon)

Mystic Willow Bay Series:

The Secret Life of a Witch

Broken Magic

Untitled (coming soon)

Standalones:

The Forgotten Girl

Honeyton Series:

The Illusion of Annabella

Rebels & Misfits Series:

Confessions of a Kleptomaniac

Rules of a Rebel and a Shy Girl

The Secrets We Carry

Untitled (coming soon)

Broken City Series:

Nameless

Forsaken

Oblivion

Forbidden (coming soon)

Sunnyvale Series:

The Year I Became Isabella Anders

The Year of Falling in Love

The Year of Second Chances

The Coincidence Series:

The Coincidence of Callie and Kayden

The Redemption of Callie and Kayden

The Destiny of Violet and Luke

The Probability of Violet and Luke

The Certainty of Violet and Luke

The Resolution of Callie and Kayden

Seth & Greyson

The Secret Series:

The Prelude of Ella and Micha

The Secret of Ella and Micha

The Forever of Ella and Micha

The Temptation of Lila and Ethan

The Ever After of Ella and Micha

Lila and Ethan: Forever and Always

Ella and Micha: Infinitely and Always

The Shattered Promises Series:

Shattered Promises

Fractured Souls

Unbroken

Broken Visions

Scattered Ashes

Breaking Nova Series:

Breaking Nova

Saving Quinton

Delilah: The Making of Red

www.ingramcontent.com/pod-product-compliance
Lightning Source LLC
Chambersburg PA
CBHW030627190726
48286CB00008B/2430